A **K.C. Flanagan, girl detective**™ adventure

CHAOS IN CANCÚN

Collect all the K.C. Flanagan, girl detective™ stories!

1. Panic in Puerto Vallarta
2. Chaos in Cancún
3. Mayhem in Maui
4. Abandoned in Aruba
5. Peril in Puerto Rico
6. Hackers From Havana

What to do if you can't find these books at your local bookstore:

A. Complain (make it loud)
B. Place a special order
C. Order from an Internet bookstore
D. Order fom the publisher (See order form at end of book)

CATALOGUING IN PUBLICATION DATA

Murray, Susan, 1960-

Chaos in Cancún
(A K.C. Flanagan, girl detective adventure ; 2)
For teenagers.

ISBN 1-55207-017-4

I. Davies, Robert, 1947-   .   II. Title   III. Series: Murray, Susan, 1960-   .

K.C. Flanagan, girl detective adventure ; 2.

PZ7.M972Ch 1998   j813'.54   C98-941271-7

Catch all the K.C. Flanagan news on the web at
http://www.rdppub.com/KookCase

Susan Murray and Robert Davies

CHAOS IN CANCÚN

ROBERT DAVIES MULTIMEDIA

Ordering information:

USA/CANADA:

General Distribution Services
1-800-387-0141/387-0172 (Canada)
1-800-805-1083 (USA)
Free Fax 1-800-481-6207
PUBNET 6307940

or from the publisher:

Robert Davies Multimedia Publishing
330-4999 St. Catherine Street West
Westmount, Que., Canada H3Z 1T3
514-481-2440 Fax 514-481-9973
e-mail: rdppub@netcom.ca

Proof-read by Alexa Leblanc, Donna Vekteris and Allyna Vineberg

Robert Davies Multimedia wishes to thank the
Canada Council for the Arts,
the SODEC (Québec) and the
Department of Canadian Heritage for their support.

Author's Introduction

Hello there. If you're reading this then you're reading my second travel diary and I guess I should introduce myself. My name is Konstantina Cassandra Flanagan, but to my way of thinking Konstantina sounds a lot like an accordion so I prefer that my friends call me K.C. I am fourteen and three quarters years old and I live in Montreal with my older brother Rudy and my father, James Flanagan, Esq. My father is a lawyer for an international construction company based here in Montreal. He travels a lot on business and so does Linda, his Significant Other. She's a freelance photo-journalist and when she and Father travel, my brother Rudy and I often get to travel with them.

Despite the fact that they named me after Mother's weird sister and despite the fact that they're now divorced (no blame on me), my parents are pretty cool people. Father's great-grandfather came from Ireland, so he's full of blarney, something of which he misguidedly claims I have inherited. Personally I think the gift of the gab helps him in his job quite a bit.

My mother's parents are from Greece, their name is Gigantes, from an old and famous Greek Jewish family whose ancestors fought the battle of Marathon. And won!

So I'm around! Mother is a sculptress and lives in both Calgary, of all places, and Dallas. She shares her life with an oil company executive named Darrell Hughes, who is actually pretty swift.

Rudy is my older brother. He's almost 18. His hobbies are sports, sports, sports and girls, girls, girls. In any order of the moment. He's actually pretty smart when he applies himself to something and like all my friends tell me, he's cute too. But don't tell him that, he already knows it! I guess he's an all right kind of brother, even if he does tease me a lot.

Anyway my point is this: I've been to a lot of really cool places and I've been keeping a diary about my travels. Some of the things that have happened to me are pretty fantastic. Rudy will tell you that I attract trouble but don't even listen to him. I mean, I guess you could say that I've been in some pretty tight spots but it's not like it's my fault. The truth is that I have a keen eye for detail and deduction. When strange things happen around me I like to investigate and find out why. I think you'll see my point when you read my story. I just got back from Cancún, Mexico, in the state of Quintana Roo, where I had one of the strangest experiences of my life.

My older brother Rudy pokes his head in the door to my room and informs me:

"I'm expecting a call from Jackie, so if she calls and you answer the phone, don't use that fake accent on her again, all right?"

"I was jus' practicin' my suhthern Amurican dialek', Roo-boy" I say with an innocent grin, but he frowns, failing to appreciate my sense of humor.

"I really mean it, K.C.," he tells me, raising his voice.

"Oh all right, Trudy,*" I reply and that does it, he leaves me alone.*

Where was I? Oh, OK, my trip to Cancún. Cancún is a city in Mexico on the coast of what's called the Yucatán Peninsula. The Yucatán is hot, flat and beautiful in a sort of tropical way, filled with the crumbling ruins of ancient Mayan cities.

If you like luxury resorts, there are lots of world-class places to stay in Cancún, but if you prefer local color I would recommend Isla Mujeres, a small island off the coast which is where we ended up staying. But I should start at the beginning, shouldn't I?

My older brother Rudy, my father, James Flanagan, and Linda Hébert, Father's 'significant other' and I went to Cancún a few months ago for a vacation.

Father works for an international construction company, and so Rudy and I often get to travel with him when he's on business, but the reason we all went to Cancún was because of Linda, who had to do research for an article she was writing about the ancient Mayan people of the Yucatán Peninsula.

We stayed on Isla Mujeres, where Julian Sayles, a famous archaeologist who Linda wanted to interview, and his crew were working on restoring the ruins of an old Mayan temple. Father, Rudy and I planned to take it easy and just relax on the beach, but of course that's not what actually happened.

Let's just say that things got a little too interesting and I ended up stuck in a — wait a second. If I tell you that part now you'll probably never read the rest of my diary.

The phone rings and I answer it quickly:

8

"Howdy y'all." *There is a brief silence, then a girl's shy voice asks,*

"Is Rudy there?" *Rudy picks up the phone, irritated now.* *"I heard that, K.C., now hang up already, it's for me."* *Gently, I put the phone down.*

Anyway, I hope you don't mind reading the rest on your own to find out what happens. I'm writing these diaries for extra credit in my English Composition class and the teacher is always telling us it's bad form to give away the ending in the introduction.

I'll add one word of caution, though. If a short, fat man in a white suit and hat with a gold and ruby pinky ring ever approaches you, just take my word for it and run away as far and as fast as you can. I think you'll see why I feel so strongly about this when you finish reading my story.

Chapter One

"The other thing I like about Pamela is that she's *so* talented," this was my brother Rudy, rhapsodizing about his girlfriend, The Lovely Pamela. "I mean, the way she handles herself in front of a crowd is awesome, don't you think, K.C.?" I sighed, thinking of Pamela's rather average cheerleading skills.

"She's OK," I replied noncommittally.

"Oh come on, she's the coolest." He said this with such indulgent patience that I didn't even bother to reply. For an entire month, everything coming out of Rudy's mouth had been 'Pamela this,' and 'Pamela that.' I was starting to feel that if he mentioned her one more time I was literally going to scream. Or maybe lock him up with a year's supply of Baywatch reruns.

"Watch out!" Rudy shouted and I pulled hard on the wheel of the golf cart I was driving, swerving just in time to avoid a collision with a girl on a moped who pulled out from a side street into the road in front of me. "That was way too close for comfort, K.C.," Rudy scolded me, even though we'd missed the girl on the moped by a good ten feet.

"But that wasn't even my fault!" I protested, "she just zoomed out in front of me — she didn't even look where she was going."

"A good driver is always aware of what is happening around her," Rudy told me primly. "You should have been ready for her." Ready for someone to dart out into traffic right in front of me when I had the right of way? I was just a beginning driver, but I did know the rules of the road.

"But...!" I began to protest until Rudy held up a hand to silence me.

"No buts. You need to pay more attention to what's happening around you, K.C." I fumed in silence, stomping the 'go' pedal to the floor in frustration. The little cart surged ahead at its top speed of ten miles an hour.

There was no way I could win. If I focused on the road ahead of me, Rudy warned me to be aware of side streets. If I watched the side streets, he told me to keep my eyes on the road. And anyway, how did he expect me to concentrate when he kept blathering on and on about The Lovely Pamela? It was enough to put anyone to sleep!

We were traveling south on Avenida Benito Juárez which hugs the east side of Isla Mujeres, a small island just across the bay from Cancún, Mexico. Father, Rudy and I were there on vacation, but for Father's girlfriend Linda it was a working trip.

Linda is a freelance photojournalist. She has one of the coolest jobs of anyone I know, because she gets paid to fly around the world and take pictures of and write about natural and historical phenomena. As a matter of fact she was in Mexico to research an article about the culture of the ancient Mayans for a prestigious travel and culture magazine.

I ignored yet another one of Rudy's tips on the finer points of driving, taking my eyes from the road in front of me to glance out over the cacti and the rocks on my left toward the sea, where three iguanas were sunning themselves on adjacent boulders, lined up in a row like soldiers at attention.

The water of the Caribbean Sea around Cancún and Isla Mujeres is gorgeous, shading from light crystal green in the shallower areas to a deep blue-green farther out to sea. I have rarely seen such heart-breakingly lovely colors anywhere else.

We passed a large, oddly-shaped white stucco building. From the back it looked like a huge white ear rising from the ground, but from the other side I could see that it was actually fashioned to resemble an enormous conch shell. The asphalt road ahead of us curved to the right sharply, and I thought I spotted the top of the lighthouse which was our destination.

Another iguana was sunning itself in the middle of the road ahead of us so I zoomed around it into the left lane, maintaining my speed.

"K.C.!" Rudy was shocked, reacting to my technique as though I were dodging in and out of oncoming traffic. "You know you're not supposed to swerve into the left lane like that! Slow down and stop if you have to, but don't drive in the left lane." I glanced sideways at him, mutinously. I love Rudy a lot but he can be a real pain sometimes.

"Fine," I said, slowing to a stop and turning the golf cart off. "How about if you drive for a while then?" To tell the truth, I felt I'd already mastered the operation of the cart, the controls were brainlessly easy. Besides, driving might keep my brother from talking.

Rudy gave me a surprised look, then shrugged and traded places with me, assuming the driver's seat with a sigh of satisfaction. I settled comfortably beside him under the shade of the canopy which topped the little cart and protected us from the sun's hot rays. Rudy started the cart by turning the key to the 'on' position and depressing the 'go' pedal.

"I must say you were doing a fine job of driving there, K.C. You were really starting to get the hang of it," he said expansively. "A little more practice and you'll be a fine driver." (Of course, Rudy only just got his driving permit the week before we left for Cancún, but why make a federal case out of it? Still...)

As he nodded condescendingly at me, a gust of wind caught the cart's canopy, lifting it slightly. Rudy hit the brakes and the cart skidded in a patch of sand on the road; for a moment it looked as though we would topple into the ditch. Rudy saved us by swerving violently into the left lane, pulling us away from the brink of disaster just in time.

"Eyes on the road," I told him crisply as he veered wildly across the asphalt, regaining control of the golf cart, "and remember, young man, please try to stay on the right side of the road where we belong."

Rudy slowed the cart to a crawl as we passed three men stacking big grey concrete bricks in the hot sun. Their project was out of sight of the road, hidden behind a large green plastic dust screen. Clouds of dust and the sound of a jackhammer arose from behind the screen. One of the workers, a boy only a little older than me, grinned and waved as we swept by. I waved back at him cheerfully.

I consulted the map then pointed to the dirt road. "I think we turn off here," I said and Rudy veered left onto the dusty track leading toward the lighthouse and the ruins of the Temple of Ixchel.

The lighthouse was not very tall, rising just about one hundred feet from the ground, but I could easily tell that there was no need for it to be an impressive structure on its own. It had the advantage of being built on white limestone cliffs which rose up hundreds of feet from the sea below and were topped by a narrow crest of wind-blown grass.

Not far past the lighthouse, at the very end of the peninsula, were the remains of the Temple of Ixchel. The temple, although no doubt impressive in its day, was now little more than a crumbling edifice of golden stone blocks.

Three people were standing around the base of the temple. I recognized my father even from a distance (his six foot height and thick reddish brown hair are distinctive anywhere). His girlfriend (or should I say, 'significant other') Linda was standing beside him, camera in one hand and tape recorder in the other.

Linda is of medium height, has long blonde hair, and is more energetic than anyone I've ever met. I like her a lot and Rudy does too. I think we're both hoping things work out for Father and Linda.

Rudy parked the golf cart near the lighthouse and we walked toward the ruins. Linda was deep in conversation with a man wearing faded blue jeans and a white work shirt stained with dust. I wondered if he was Julian Sayles, the world-renowned archaeologist whom Linda had come here to interview.

"*¡Hola!*" I shouted, waving to Father and Linda. Father waved back and I jumped up and down, happy as a puppy in the warm sun.

"¡Hola K.C.!" Father waved Rudy and me over and introduced us. "Julian, these are my two children, Rudy and K.C. "Kids, I'd like you to meet the famous Julian Sayles."

I studied the man as I shook hands with him, surprised to find that the Yucatán's most renowned archaeologist was much younger than I'd expected him to be. He couldn't have been much more than thirty years of age and instead of being the stoop-shouldered scholar I'd expected to meet he was muscular, of medium height, with a mop of curly brown hair.

"Pleased to meet you, Mr. Sayles," I said formally, and he smiled back at me.

"Pleased to meet you, Rudy, K.C." He nodded politely, and shook hands with each of us in turn. "Please call me Julian."

"How was the trip over here?" Linda addressed Rudy over her shoulder but included me in her glance. "Did you show K.C. how to drive the golf cart?" I rolled my eyes at her behind Rudy's back and grimaced as he answered her question somewhat pompously:

"K.C. still has a lot to learn about the finer points of driving but in time and with practice I think she'll get the hang of it." Linda grinned at me conspiratorially.

"It's nice of you to take her under your wing like this, Rudy," she told him gravely, a wicked twinkle in her eyes as she studied my resentful expression, "K.C. is lucky to have a big brother who's willing to help her out like you have." Rudy's head expanded visibly under all this praise.

"It's no trouble at all, really," he allowed kindly, "I was a beginner once, too, it's something we all have to go through."

"I've been interviewing Julian about the work he's been doing here at the Temple of Ixchel," Linda informed us. "He and his crew are doing an absolutely fantastic job of restoring the temple, aren't they?" I eyed the rather unimpressive heap of rocks a few feet away doubtfully.

"Restoration?" I asked politely. Julian looked at me with a twinkle in his blue eyes.

"Not much to look at, is it?" he asked me, and I glanced at him, startled that he had read my thoughts.

"Well, no," I admitted, "it's not," and Julian laughed.

"This site was much more impressive before it was flattened by Hurricane Gilbert in 1988. I know it doesn't look like much, but it's really a very significant site, archaeologically speaking. The ancient Mayans used to stop here on Isla Mujeres as they made their pilgrimage to Cozumel," he explained.

"I see." I studied the ruins with renewed interest, remembering what I had learned of Ixchel, Mayan Goddess of the Moon. She represented fertility, medicine, and healing.

I stepped closer to the ancient temple and noticed that the blocks of stone lying on the ground around it were in ordered rows, each had its own number painted in white on it, probably to indicate their order of re-assembly into the blocks which were still standing.

"Want to check it out?" Julian asked, and when I nodded he added, "Watch your step near the wall, there — it's a long way down," pointing to the cliffs which fell away on either side of the ruins.

I looked down at waves crashing against jagged black rocks several hundred feet below. There were no guard rails or hand ropes to keep us away from the edge and from what could be a devastating fall hundreds of feet down.

We caught up with Father, Rudy and Linda at the tip of the peninsula where Linda was adjusting her camera for a panoramic shot of the sea.

I wandered away from them and cautiously approached the far southeastern edge of the cliff, looking down at the wide expanse of the Caribbean Sea below.

I could see why the people of the island had found it necessary to build a lighthouse on this stretch of rock. The rocks in the water below looked treacherous and I could easily imagine ships coming to grief among them.

A flash of color down where the waves were battering the cliffs caught my eye and I frowned, staring down intently. At first I thought it had been my imagination and that there was nothing there, but then I saw it again, a flash of orange from something apparently lodged in the rocks at the bottom of the cliff.

Chapter Two

I crept closer to the edge of the cliff, reaching for my binoculars and peering down in fascination. What appeared to be an orange buoy bobbed violently atop the waves below me, a marker for what, I couldn't imagine.

"Careful," Julian said, as he grabbed my arm and pulled me gently back from the edge of the cliff. "The wind can be pretty strong at this height. You don't want it to take you by surprise up here." His blue eyes were friendly and frank.

"I saw something down there," I told him as he released my arm.

"Oh?" he said, his dark brows arching upward in surprise. "What?" I shook my head, frowning.

"I couldn't quite make it out, but there seemed to be an orange buoy down there, by the cliffs."

"That's not possible," he told me gently. "Those rocks are off limits, they're far too dangerous for people to approach and no reason for a buoy. It must have been a piece of flotsam." Rudy had strolled over to join us in time to catch Julian's remark.

"Seeing things again, Kook Case?" he asked me, offering a commiserating smile to Julian. "Don't mind my little sister, Julian. She's got an over-active imagination."

"I do not!" I protested.

"We all have our little idiosyncrasies," Julian commented obliquely and, giving me a crooked sideways smile took my arm gently once more, steering me further away from the edge of the cliff. I thought that my little spat with Rudy had gone unnoticed, but then I saw Linda eyeing both of us thoughtfully.

"How about if Rudy and your father drive back to the hotel in one cart and you and Julian and I take the other cart? I'd love to hear about your day, honey," Linda suggested. Julian and I exchanged friendly glances.

"It's all right with me," I agreed.

"No problem," Julian said, and handed her the keys to the cart. "Is it all right if you drive, Linda? I have a few notes to make on our progress today."

"Oh, but I might want to take pictures or write things down," Linda replied, holding the keys out to me. "How about you. K.C., you up for driving?"

"Sure," I smiled, happily accepting the keys.

Julian took the passenger seat and Linda sat behind me as I started the cart. The little engine sputtered to life, noisy but not noisy enough to prohibit conversation.

Julian pulled a small black notebook out of his shirt pocket and jotted something in it as I guided the cart along the road back to Isla Mujeres, following Rudy and Father. After he finished writing he turned to Linda and me with a smile.

"So, how do you like Isla Mujeres?"

"It's paradise," I told him quite sincerely, "glorious and quiet." In fact, the island was about as relaxed a place as anywhere I'd ever been.

Not that I was complaining, mind you. My last 'vacation' with Rudy and Father several months ago in

Puerto Vallarta had turned into a "bang-bang" adventure as I'd tangled with a nasty drug smuggler. As far as I was concerned, peace and quiet were far preferable to that kind of action any day.

"Not much happens here," Julian shrugged. "It's not a big center of commerce or anything. The main industries here are tourism and fishing." I nodded. The small town of Isla Mujeres was popular as a jumping-off point for tourists heading out to Cancún, Cozumel and Chichén Itzá.

"What does Isla Mujeres mean, anyway?" I asked Julian curiously.

"It means Isle of Women," he told me, "the Spanish conquistadors named it when they first came to the Yucatán Peninsula in 1517."

"Why?" I asked, "were there a bunch of Amazon women living here or something?" Julian laughed.

"No. It's probably because when the Conquistadors arrived they found a lot of clay figures of women on the island, probably left behind by the Mayans as offerings to Ixchel." Linda shot him a smile.

"Other people say it's because this is where the Spanish buccaneers used to keep their women, um —" she stopped in mid-sentence, and out of the corner of my eye I saw her glance at me.

"Mistresses?" I supplied the missing word and Linda shrugged, then nodded.

"Well, captives, prisoners of war, ladies, you know," she finished somewhat lamely, obviously deeming a more colorful description to be unsuitable for one of my tender years.

"Spanish buccaneers huh?" I repeated. "You mean, as in pirates?" There was a short pause and then Julian answered me.

"This island is famous for having once been a stopping point for Spanish slave traders and pirates, yes."

"The entire Yucatán coast was frequented by merchants and pirates in the mid 1500's, wasn't it?" Linda asked and Julian nodded in response.

I concentrated on driving while Julian and Linda talked about the history of the Spanish invasion of Mexico.

In 1517 Francisco Hernández de Cordova was the first official Spaniard to see the 'New World,' as South America was considered by Europeans. His discovery was followed by increasing interest from Spain, which in 1519 sent Hernán Cortés to buy Mayan slaves.

Eight years after that Francisco Montejo and his son had traveled inland, taking the Yucatán by force.

The Spanish conquest of the Mayan people was aided by the diseases the Spaniards had brought with them. Huge numbers of the Mayan people were believed to have been wiped out by smallpox, chicken pox and influenza, making the conquest a simple matter of medical fact.

"Like the black plague," Linda commented, taking notes as Julian went on.

"About as devastating to the Mayan population, yes," Julian confirmed.

We were more than halfway back to the town of Isla Mujeres and were passing what looked like a private airstrip on our right side. I wanted to study it more closely, along with the fairly posh neighborhood surrounding it, but traffic was picking up now so I stayed alert.

"What were the Mayas like?" I asked, "before the Spanish came, I mean." I'd done a little reading on the subject myself but was still interested in hearing his opinion.

"Have you been to see any of the nearby Mayan ruins yet?" he answered my question with one of his own and I shook my head.

"No, why?"

"It would be easier to explain them if you had." He looked over his shoulder at Linda and asked, "Why don't we all go see Chichén Itzá together tomorrow? Are you free?" Linda's face lit up.

"Really?" She was obviously trying not to gush. "That would be great, Julian. I'll have to talk to James about it but as far as this article is concerned it would be best if I could interview you right at the location of your discovery."

"Discovery?" I repeated curiously. Linda leaned forward to explain:

"Julian was restoring part of the ancient city of Chichén Itzá and he discovered a stone calendar indicating the beginning of Mayan time. It is one of the most significant archaeological discoveries in recent years, K.C."

"Wow," I said, deeply impressed. Julian shot me a bemused glance.

"One of the calendars used by the ancient Mayas is called the long count and dates back to 3114 B.C.," Julian explained. "We don't know why they chose that date, but it was very significant to them for some reason."

We were approaching the outskirts of the town of Isla Mujeres and driving required all of my concentration so I stopped talking. I was sharing the road with a chaotic jumble of pedestrians, sunburned tourists in swimsuits, mopeds, taxis and other golf carts.

If we had been somewhere else in the world, in Florida for example, the chaos would have been annoying, but this was Isla Mujeres; here it was cool, people were relaxed and in no particular hurry. Instead of the impatience which is common in congested areas, there were smiles as each one waited courteously for the other to pass or turn in a display of civility too often absent from North American city driving.

I turned right at Matamoros and drove three blocks to the hotel Vista Del Mar. It was an easy building to spot from a distance, owing mostly to the fact that it was painted a deep aqua color, with dusky pink and purple balconies wrapped around the open front of the building.

Many of the buildings on Isla Mujeres were ultra-colorful and had brightly patterned awnings which served to shade the narrow sidewalks below and the pedestrians there. Still, a lot of people strolled along right in the middle of the street, making it a real challenge for me to maneuver the golf cart safely among them.

When we reached the hotel I turned into the small courtyard in back and parked there. Luis, the man at the reception desk, took the keys from me with a smile. Father and Rudy were already inside the hotel, waiting for us in the lobby.

"Meet for dinner later?" Julian directed the question at Linda and after a quick glance at my father who nodded, Linda replied:

"Sure, the buffet is at eight." Julian nodded, collected his mail and headed upstairs to the apartment he and the other members of his crew were sharing.

"Well," Father said as we took the stairs up to our own apartment. "What do you think?"

"It's hot," Rudy replied fervently, fanning himself with a magazine.

"He's nice," Linda replied.

"About what?" I asked. Father led us down a long, mauve hallway with a pink tiled floor toward a narrow stairway arching up.

"About Isla Mujeres," Father clarified, unlocking the door which led to our apartment. We were staying for a whole week and so, instead of renting single rooms, Father and Linda had decided to take advantage of the fact that the Hotel Vista Del Mar also offered spacious family apartments for short term rent.

"The island is cool," I answered, following Rudy inside the foyer. The living room was quite large, and very colorful. The walls were pale aqua, the floor was tiled in deep blue-green, and most of the wooden furniture had been painted in black enamel. The instant he'd seen it Rudy had developed a fixation about the centerpiece of the room, a puffy purple sofa embroidered with a flamboyant red floral pattern.

"So, was Julian how you expected him to be?" Father asked Linda with curiousity as she tossed her straw hat on the hat stand and headed for the kitchen. Rudy sat gingerly on the sofa, eyeing it briefly as though uncertain if it were friend or foe, then switched on the TV.

"Not really," Linda replied from the kitchen, where she got a bottle of iced tea from the refrigerator, "although I guess I'd expected him to be a little more stuffy than he is. Anyone else want some tea?"

"Me," I answered quickly. The tropical sun made me thirsty.

"I'd like one," Father added.

"Me too," Rudy spoke up and Linda returned a moment later, bearing chilled bottles of iced tea which she handed around.

I waited until everyone had had a minute to sip their tea, then announced: "Julian had a great idea for tomorrow."

Father quirked an eyebrow at me. "What's that?"

"It's about Chichén Itzá," Linda explained. "He suggested that we go to the ruins tomorrow, and offered to give us a tour of the site."

"Sounds like a good idea. What do you think, Rudy?" Father asked, raising an eyebrow in his best Irish manner.

"Fine with me," Rudy answered.

"Let's do it then," Father said. Linda's grin lit up the room.

"Oh, James," she went to give him a big hug, burying her face in his chest, "you're such a doll." He gave her a tender smile and they kissed, right in front of us! It can be a little disconcerting the way they carry on like that, I mean, they've been dating for two years but they still act like smitten teenagers.

Rudy and I never really talked about it but I think we both assume they will get married someday, although they don't seem to be in any big hurry to formally tie the knot. Linda has her own apartment in Montreal, where she lives when she's not traveling on business and Father enjoys his independence too. For now, they seem pretty happy with the way things are.

Tactfully, Rudy and I strolled out and up onto the paved rooftop of the hotel, an open expanse which stretched along one side of our apartment like a private garden. There was a fountain up there, three large potted palms and several wicker chairs in a cluster near a round wooden picnic table.

Rudy and I stood there in silence, watching as the sun set over the sea, the blue-green sky deepening into midnight blue over the velvet water which washed in gentle waves onto the white sand. Five little boys were playing soccer in a circle on the beach, kicking the ball back and forth and laughing when the ball rolled close to the waves.

"I wonder what she's doing right now," Rudy murmured, his eyes on the soccer game, his thoughts obviously elsewhere.

"Pamela," I said with resignation. It was the only word which could get through to Rudy.

"She's great, isn't she." He said it with such conviction that I knew contradicting him would only result in serious discord. I just nodded, sinking into one of the wicker chairs, and as if on cue, Rudy took the chair opposite me and leaned forward with an earnest look.

"What if she meets someone else while I'm here?" he asked, and I shook my head gently, trying hard not to be impatient with him. I would have been more sympathetic toward Rudy, but this had been going on for a month and it was getting a little stale.

"Then she isn't right for you," I replied simply. Rudy's worried look increased slightly so I pointed out reasonably, "Look, Rudy, we'll only be here for a week. Then we'll head home and everything will be fine." His face brightened then sank.

"A lot can happen in a week," he sighed heavily, his shoulders slumping. Patiently, I decided to try another approach.

"Look, Rudy, you're a cool guy, what girl could possibly forget you in one week?" A small smile crossed his face.

"That's true," he admitted self-consciously. The sound of laughter drew our attention back to the room where Father and Linda were seated side by side on the sofa, laughing together at something she had just said.

"They're so happy," Rudy's wistful look returned. "I wish Pamela were here now."

"Well she's not, so snap out of it, all right?" My small reserve of sibling understanding was gone and Rudy turned a look of hurt surprise on me at my harsh words. I sighed, "I'm sorry Rudy, it's just that you've been going on and on about Pamela for weeks now and —." Rudy held up a hand, deeply injured.

"Never mind K.C. I can see you're just too young to understand." He left me with pained dignity, heading for his own room, and I watched him go with mingled pity and frustration.

It wasn't like Rudy to mope, but he was definitely moping. I was starting to feel a little worried about him but I really couldn't think of anything to do to help him snap out of it. And after his response to my latest advice I had to admit that tough love wasn't the best way to go.

I got up and wandered downstairs, strolling one block toward the deserted end of the north beach. For a while I stood and watched the waves roll in and then I noticed a large white yacht docked at one of two long concrete piers stretching out from shore. I contemplated it curiously.

I was pretty sure the yacht hadn't been there earlier in the day, I knew I would have remembered seeing it if it had been. I studied the big vessel closely, she was about seventy-five feet long, enameled white with gold trim. There might have been the gleam of a satellite dish on the top deck. I walked closer, intrigued.

A movement caught my eye and as I watched, a short, husky man in a white suit and panama hat strode into view. He paced across the deck to stand at the side of the railing, looking expectantly toward shore as though waiting for someone. He didn't notice me standing there, but something about him made me feel uneasy. Without even knowing why I shivered as I watched him turn away abruptly, his attention caught by a second man I now saw walking down the length of the pier to board the yacht.

The first man, the one in white, now had his back to me as he stood on deck talking to the newcomer who was wearing faded blue jeans and a nondescript soiled white work shirt. I could see his face and studied it closely.

He looked like he was about thirty-five years old or so, with thick blond hair cut stylishly short and a handsome, rugged face. As I watched, the man in white reached into his breast pocket and pulled out a fat manila envelope. I caught the glint of gold on an unusual pinky ring the man in white was wearing and frowned, wondering where I had seen that ring before. I took another step toward the pier, watching as the second man took the envelope and lifted the flap. He peered inside with a twisted smile, then glanced around furtively and stuffed the envelope hastily into the pocket of his pants. He left quickly without any goodbyes, hurrying back the way he'd come. The man in white turned to watch his progress, looking straight at me, and I gasped as he turned enough for me to get a clear look at his face.

It was a face I recognized from my recent experiences on the other side of Mexico, in the Pacific coast resort town of Puerto Vallarta, and although I had only seen its owner briefly, it was a face I would never forget. The man was Señor Hernán Colón, a notoriously corrupt member of the Mexican government who had been indicted on charges of protecting a ring of drug smugglers in Puerto Vallarta. He had fled Mexico for Ireland and then to Canada after his nefarious activities had been uncovered, but was extradited back to Mexico to face charges after I recognized him in Montreal.

Since I was one of the people who had been instrumental in bringing him to justice, you can imagine the shock of fear I felt at seeing him here on Isla Mujeres, when he was supposed to be in jail pending trial.

For a split second we stared at each other, mutual recognition crackling between us like a current of electricity, then Señor Colón shouted something unintelligible and pointed at me, his face contorting with rage as yet another man appeared from the inside of the yacht's cabin.

I watched in horror as the third man listened to Colón's shouted instructions then turned and sprinted toward the pier, heading in my direction. It was clear he was coming for me and although I had no way of knowing what his intentions were I had a definite feeling that he didn't mean to engage me in a simple chat about the weather.

I took off, running as fast as I could toward the concrete promenade ahead of me through thick white sand which slowed me despite my best efforts at speed. After about fifty yards I glanced over my shoulder, hoping that I had lost my pursuer, but he was hot on my trail, in fact he was gaining on me.

Sheer terror lent wings to my feet and when I reached the concrete promenade I sprinted through the small crowd of people gathered there to view the sunset, ignoring their stares as I headed for the safety of the jumble of houses about one hundred yards away.

From the commotion behind me it was evident that I was still being pursued so I didn't waste time looking over my shoulder but turned down a small side street, weaving in and out of the vendors' stalls, past rows of colorful hand-painted masks and ceramics. At some other time I might have paused to admire the art but I could hear the slap of my pursuer's feet on the cobblestones as he came after me through the crowd.

Despite the safety my hotel represented, I knew it would be foolish for me to head straight back there, since the last thing I wanted was for Señor Colón to know where I was staying (We were registered at the hotel under Linda's name, so Colón wouldn't be able to trace me directly).

I turned two corners in rapid succession and darted into the secluded courtyard of a private residence where I crouched behind a potted palm, watching for the seconds it took my pursuer to sprint past my hiding place and disappear down the street.

After I was sure he was gone I stood up shakily and looked around at the stupefied stares of an elderly couple who had evidently been sitting down to dinner in the quiet privacy of their own home before being rudely interrupted by my intrusion.

"Um, *lo siento, señora, señor,*" I shrugged and spread my hands, indicating that it had all been a mistake and that I was sorry to have disturbed them. "I'm sorry, please forgive me." The elderly man at the table exchanged puzzled glances with his wife who turned to me with a cool shrug, motioning away the impolite *gringa*. "I'll just be on my way now," I added apologetically, skulking back into the street.

I walked quickly back to the hotel Vista Del Mar, peering around myself every few steps for fear that I might again encounter Colón's henchman. The scariest part of the whole thing was wondering what Señor Colón was doing on Isla Mujeres in the first place, when he was supposed to be safely locked up in Mexico City.

That he had recognized me as I had recognized him was undeniable and it seemed clear from his reaction that he was not at all happy with my presence on the island. Dejectedly, I turned into the stairs leading to the veranda of the hotel, casting one last look over my shoulder to be certain I was unobserved before heading upstairs to tell Father what I had seen. I found him on the roof, looking for me.

Chapter Three

"Ready for dinner?" Father called cheerfully, then his eyes got all concerned and he added, "is everything all right, sweetheart?" I shook my head breathlessly.

"Dad, I just saw Señor Colón, he was on a yacht at the beach and when he saw me he made some guy chase me all over town!" I knew I was babbling but couldn't help myself. Father gave me a strange look and put an arm gently across my shoulders.

"K.C. honey, it couldn't possibly have been him. Señor Colón is in jail right now, you know that." His tone was patient and very understanding but I shook my head vehemently.

"It was him, I recognized him from Puerto Vallarta, and from when we ran into him in Montreal. Dad, he was wearing that same odd ring!" Father hugged me reassuringly.

"K.C., it's getting dark, and visibility is limited. You probably saw someone who looked like him and even dressed like him, but I know for a fact that right now Señor Colón is behind bars." He gave me a compassionate look, but something in his tone made me feel like a little kid again.

"Then why did that guy chase me like that?" I asked stubbornly. Father sighed and tipped my chin up gently, looking me right in the eyes.

"Probably because you were trespassing on private property. You were, weren't you?" True, in all likelihood I *had* been trespassing, but Father was missing the point. Before I could protest further he continued, "Listen, K.C., you had a pretty rough time in Puerto Vallarta and it's only natural that you'll be nervous for a while. Go easy on yourself." He released me gently and tousled my hair, smiling at Linda and Rudy who I realized were watching us from the doorway.

"I'm sorry, maybe you're right, but it did look like him," I muttered.

"Don't worry about it, K.C.," Father replied lovingly, it's no big deal."

Rudy, however, was not so kind. "Is our little K.C. seeing things again?" he smiled sarcastically, shaking his head a little. "What was it this time? A UFO?" I knew that the real reason he was being mean was because I'd cheesed him off about The Lovely Pamela so I ignored his jibe, in the fashion of the truly mature. More mature than him, anyway.

"K.C. thought she saw Señor Colón on a yacht," Father murmured to Linda who gave me a sympathetic smile.

"Oh, how scary for you, honey. What did he look like?"

"Short, husky, wearing a white suit. And I didn't just *think* I saw him, it was really him, please, Linda, don't you believe me?"

To my chagrin she just shook her head, and said, "I believe that *you* believe you saw him, every one of us has a double somewhere, including Señor Colón. But it couldn't really be him because Señor Colón is in jail. His trial comes up in three weeks, isn't that right James?" Linda turned to Father and he nodded.

"Two, actually."

Linda shrugged. "So you see, K.C., it couldn't have been him. But I don't blame you for being nervous. If everything that happened to you in Puerto Vallarta had happened to me I'd be looking over my shoulder for months."

Well, that was a candid admission, and I hugged her, smiling a little. It was true that I'd been pretty antsy lately.

I looked at the faces of my beloved family. From the concerned looks they were giving me I could tell that protesting any more would only make things worse. Still, I couldn't help adding again, a trifle sulkily, "Well, I may be jumpy but I'm not crazy, you know."

"Of course you aren't," Father added. "You know we're here for you if you feel like talking, honey," and I could tell from his tone that I'd been the subject of previous discussions. No doubt he and Linda were worried about whether or not I'd been psychologically damaged by my experience in Puerto Vallarta. Post traumatic stress syndrome, I think they call it. Well, when a brutally handsome psychopathic drug smuggler named Ravalos threatens to blow your brains out in Puerto Vallarta, I guess that qualifies as stressful. On the other hand though, he's the one in a Mexican jail for life now, so maybe he's the one that needs stress therapy!

Still, I had the feeling that if I wasn't careful, I would end up spending some of my summer vacation in the air-conditioned office of a psychiatrist so I decide not to push the issue any further.

"It doesn't help that K.C. goes out of her way to look for trouble," Rudy pointed out scornfully, miffed at the special treatment I was getting. I shot him an annoyed glance.

I don't go 'looking for trouble' *Trudy*," I told him angrily. "I'm sorry I thought I saw Colón and ruined your day. I guess I was mistaken, as usual!"

"Well, I'd appreciate it if you'd just try to get a grip for the rest of the week because *some* of us want to relax and have a normal vacation for a change, *Kookcase*," he snapped back.

"Fine with me!" I glanced up, clenching my teeth, but when I caught Father and Linda's twin stares of disapproval over this childish quarrel I changed gears and added sweetly, "Don't mind Rudy, he's just cranky because he's going through *witch*drawal. Oh, I mean *with*drawal, of course."

"Withdrawal? From what?" Linda looked concerned and she shot a startled glance at Rudy as I added:

"From The Lovely Pamela, of course. Two more days without her, I guarantee he'll be a basket case." I stage-whispered this but Rudy overheard and scowled at me.

"Leave Pamela out of this, K.C., she doesn't have anything to do with it. The problem is you and your childish obsession with solving mysteries!" Linda held up a hand, looking from Rudy to me.

"Kids," she began tactfully.

"That's exactly my point!" I retorted, fed up with Rudy's overbearingly superior attitude. "For someone as childishly obsessed as you are, you have a heck of a nerve pointing it out in others!"

"Me?" Rudy was momentarily taken aback. "I am not obsessed!"

"You are too! Every other word is 'Pamela this, Pamela that', it's driving us all crazy!"

"That's enough now, kids." When Father uses that tone with us, both Rudy and I know better than to say another word. "I want you both to just simmer down while we have dinner, with not another word out of either of you unless it's something nice. Got it?" Rudy and I nodded but glared mutinously at each other. Father sighed and shot a quick glance at Linda who put in:

"I think you've both made your points anyway. Rudy, you're right. Sometimes K.C. is a little," Linda smiled at me, "imaginative." Rudy gave me a triumphant smile as she continued, "but her point is valid too. You do spend a lot of time talking about Pamela lately." Linda stopped and looked at us.

"We all have a quirk or two, don't we? But that's just part of being a family," Father squinted thoughtfully at Linda as she continued, "We learn to live with our differences. There's enough room for everyone if we can all exercise a little respect." I glanced at Rudy warily and he shrugged, looking away as Father chimed in:

"That's a very good way for you two to look at it. Rudy, try to keep in mind that as outrageous as some of K.C.'s observations are, she's often right and you, K.C., you have to remember that love is a complex emotion, it can make men do strange and wonderful things." Father smiled and glanced at Linda who blushed and started fiddling with the silver bracelet she'd bought earlier in the day.

"So," Father smiled broadly, obviously pleased with his own parenting skills, "are we all friends again?" Rudy and I eyed each other simultaneously, nodding blandly.

"Fine," Rudy smiled cagily, showing all of his teeth.

"Right," I smiled back, just as carefully.

"Let's go have some dinner." Tactfully changing the subject, Father led us downstairs to meet Julian and the rest of his crew at their table in the neighboring Restaurant Carola, where they had been sipping beer in the tropical evening.

"Linda, James, here we are." Julian waved us over cheerily and we joined him, sliding into empty seats around the table. Julian caught my eye and smiled as he introduced the two men with him. "These are my associates and fellow archaeologists, Beau Cooper and Billy Joe Walton."

Despite the fact that we were already seated, the one named Billy Joe waved a mug of beer at us, spilling half of it onto the plastic table cloth in front of him as he shouted, "Hey, pull up a chair!" When I looked at his face closely I felt a stab of sudden fear.

I'd had a very clear look at the man who had joined Señor Colón on the yacht and it had definitely been Billy Joe. He had changed his soiled work shirt for a fresh white one but seemed to be wearing the same dusty jeans. He didn't seem to recognize me though, and I watched him warily, wondering what his connection to Señor Colón could be while Billy Joe dabbed ineffectually at the table before him, managing to slop quite a bit of beer onto Linda's lap.

"Sorry about your dress," Billy Joe said, eyeing Linda's outfit intently. It might have been my imagination but it seemed to me that his speech was a little slurred. I saw Father come to the same conclusion and he met my eyes briefly before turning a thoughtful gaze on Billy Joe and draping an arm casually around Linda's shoulders.

"So, how do you like the island so far?" I was sitting next to Beau and he was polite enough to make small talk. I studied him surreptitiously. His accent told me he was American, probably from somewhere in the southern United States, maybe Louisiana or Florida.

"It's great here," I replied simply, "don't you agree?" Up close, I could see a faint scar on his lip which twisted his mouth into a perpetually mocking smile; like everyone else on the island (except perhaps me) he was tanned a deep walnut brown by the hours he'd spent working in the sun helping Julian rebuild Ixchel's temple.

"It's OK," Beau shrugged noncommittally, "can't criticize paradise, can we kid?"

"You can call me K.C.," I said politely.

"What's that stand for?" Beau asked me curiously and I hesitated a moment then told him.

"Konstantina Cassandra," I replied warily. He considered it for a moment then shook his head.

"You think that's bad?" he lowered his voice confidentially. "Try Evelyn Beauregard Cooper." I would have smiled but I know first hand how it feels to be teased for something you can't do anything about, like what you were named.

"Evelyn? That really is quite a name," I deadpanned.

"Tell me about it," he shook his head ruefully. "Man, did I ever get into some fights as a kid."

After a while the waiter came over to take our orders and across the table Billy Joe held up his hand, waggling two fingers to attract his attention. I saw Julian look at him with concern.

"Another beer, with a shot of tequila on the side," Billy Joe ordered and Julian exchanged a sharp glance with Beau who shook his head slightly. The waiter hurried off and returned a moment later with another big mug of *cerveza*, which he set down in front of Billy Joe.

"So," Linda spoke up, easing the tension, "you three guys have been working together for a few years, isn't that right?" Julian nodded in reply.

"Beau and Billy Joe were with me at Chichén Itzá, when we found the calendar." At Julian's words I thought the three men exchanged swift, tense glances. Then the moment passed and Billy Joe took a noisy pull at his beer, accidentally inhaling some of it in his haste. For a moment no one spoke as Billy Joe coughed and gurgled, pounding on his own chest with both hands.

"I hate when that happens!" he announced once he had recovered. Linda ignored him, smiling at Julian encouragingly.

"How long have you guys been working here on the island?"

Julian gave Linda a strained smile, keeping a wary eye on Billy Joe who had settled down to do some serious damage to his drinks. "In two weeks it will be four months. We had hoped to finish sooner but the ruins were in such a state of disrepair it's been necessary for us to replace much of the missing masonry by creating it ourselves." Linda nodded.

"I wouldn't be surprised if a lot of the temple bricks were washed right into the sea at the base of the cliff. Did you ever go down there and look for them?" she asked. Julian's eyes narrowed.

"It's far too dangerous down there, the force of the water against the rocks would be enough to crush anyone who tried to dive down there, that's for sure."

"Yeah," Billy Joe added, a little too loudly, "it's a real crap shoot down there, lemme tell you we —" Billy Joe jumped suddenly in his seat, and winced as though he'd been jolted. Someone's leg brushed mine under the table and I squinted sideways at Beau, wondering if he had just kicked Billy Joe.

"Sorry," Beau apologized courteously. Billy Joe muttered something unintelligible yet clearly resentful, rubbing at his knee under the table.

"Anyway, the point is, the project is going to take much longer than we thought," Julian finished smoothly, giving us all little reassuring glances as if to distract us from Billy Joe's bizarre behavior.

"Is the work you're doing on the temple anything like the work you did at Chichén Itzá?" Father asked politely. Julian considered the question then shook his head.

"In a way, yes, but also very different. Chichén Itzá was much easier because the pieces of the temple are all mostly there; it's just a matter of finding and reassembling them. Ixchel's temple needs complete rebuilding though, and that's what's slowing us down." Billy Joe took another long pull of beer and blinked owlishly at the rest of us as he leaned confidingly toward Linda.

"Damn generator broke," he muttered roughly. "That slowed us down consid'rably but hell, it's worth it, we hit the jackpot, didn't we?" Billy Joe smiled broadly at Julian and Beau, lifting his glass to his associates and winking as he toasted them. "Here's to scientific discovery." Linda nodded uncertainly, glancing around at the rest of us who were watching this exchange with mingled fascination and embarrassment.

"Time to go, pal." Seizing Billy Joe by the shoulders, Beau pulled him firmly to his feet, addressing the rest of us with a slightly sheepish smile: "You'll have to forgive Billy Joe, folks, it's been a long day and we didn't have much to eat in the way of lunch."

"Hey, let go!" Billy Joe said as he lurched away and brushed himself off, hands fumbling a little. "I'm fine, just a little tired is all." He frowned at us all, trying for dignified self-control then belched loudly, totally ruining the effect. Rudy met my eyes for a brief second then we both looked away quickly. It didn't take Sherlock Holmes to deduce that Billy Joe had had way too much to drink.

"That's all right buddy, we're just going to go upstairs and get some sleep." Beau steered him firmly away from the table and the rest of us stared at one another silently for a long, tense moment.

"He'll be fine in the morning." Julian's voice was hearty but there was a strained quality to his smile, as though he were failing to see the situation in its most amusing light.

"He may have a touch of heat stroke," Linda suggested. We all gazed at her in surprise. That's one of the things I love about Linda. She will always give a person the benefit of the doubt, even when there is substantial evidence to the contrary. "Well, it's possible," she defended herself although no one had said a word and we all hid our smiles. The tension eased after that though, and we went back to our food.

"So, what was it that you guys found?" I asked Julian cheerfully, referring to Billy Joe's reference to hitting the 'jackpot.' Julian coughed on a sip of water, and it was a moment before he could reply.

"Nothing," he told me, patting his lips delicately with his napkin. I watched as he refolded it neatly, placing it carefully by his plate.

"But he said you hit the jackpot, the scientific discovery thing." I reminded him and Julian snapped his fingers, realization dawning in his eyes.

"Wait. He probably meant that carving of Ixchel we uncovered," his tone was thoughtful, "but it wasn't a very significant find, not really."

"Carving?" Linda asked, her professional interest piqued.

Julian nodded. "Yeah, the carving. Of Ixchel," he added, perhaps picturing it in his mind's eye, "it was pretty beat up."

"Could I see it sometime?" Linda was clearly excited, "I'd love to include it in the article."

"We'll see," Julian shook his head gravely. "But you know, there are very strict laws about what happens to artifacts here. We have to keep track of everything we find and report it to the Mexican government."

"How come?" I asked, curious.

"There was an incredible scandal in the 1960's when an archaeologist made off with the contents of the sacrificial well at Chichén Itzá. Ever since then," he said ruefully, "we're required to turn everything we find over to the authorities. You'd have to come back to the temple and—"

"I don't mind a bit," Linda smiled brightly. "The carving would be a good feature for the part of the story about your discoveries. I'll visit the site sometime later this week," she beamed at Julian.

"Is the statue valuable?" I asked and Julian shrugged, leaning back in his chair.

"Hard to say, it might be."

"I'd like to see it too," I nodded at Linda. I thought I saw a shadow cross Julian's face. He must have sensed my eyes on him then for he glanced up at me and smiled warmly.

It was the kind of smile you share with an old friend and I smiled back at him without reservation. Rudy looked from me to Julian then back at me, and under his speculative gaze I confess I blushed a little.

Julian rose to his feet. "I should be going," he said, "are we still on for tomorrow? We'll need to get an early start if we want to make it all the way to Chichén Itzá and back before dark." Although his words were directed at Linda they were meant for all of us.

"Absolutely," I put in before Linda could reply, ignoring Rudy's knowing smirk.

"Shall we say six o'clock then? In the lobby?" Julian grinned at my look of dismay. I am not what you could call a morning person and for me getting out of bed at six a.m. is a challenge I undertake only for the very worthiest of causes.

"Six will be fine," Father replied for all of us, which was good because personally I doubt I could have forced the words out.

"See you then," Julian said and left us.

"K.C. has a crush on Julian," Rudy remarked loudly. Fortunately Julian was well out of earshot.

"I do not!" I was outraged by his mistaken assumption, "just because *you* have 'love' on the brain you assume everyone else does too!"

"I saw the way you were looking at him," Rudy informed me smugly.

"Oh yeah? Now *you're* the one who's seeing things, Trudy," I knew full well that I had conducted myself with dignity and maturity. Any interest I had shown in Julian was due to my fascination with archaeology. That was clear as a bell to me. I guess.

"Julian seems like a very interesting person," Linda put in tactfully, trying to catch Rudy's eye in order to give him a warning look. "K.C. could learn a lot from him." Rudy grinned, unabashed.

"Yeah, first love is always so instructive."

"You should talk," I shook my head in disgust. Rudy had a lot of nerve accusing *me* of love-struck behavior.

"It's true and you know it," he said, folding his arms on his chest.

"Is not," I shot right back, staring him down.

"Let's not fight about love, all right kids?" Father interjected a little sadly, "but since you two are bickering all the time like the Odd Couple, why don't you see if you can work out your differences like adults?"

"Yeah, Rudy, grow up," I scolded him, "try acting your age instead of your shoe size for a change."

"Grow up yourself, Kook Case," he retorted and Father sighed, glancing at Linda in resignation.

"How about if we all go get some sleep, since we're getting up so early," Linda suggested diplomatically and at that, Father got to his feet.

We paid the bill for dinner and went upstairs to the apartment, where we quickly disbanded and went into our own rooms. So much for after-dinner family bonding.

While I got ready for bed, showering and brushing my hair, I wondered what to do about the situation. Father and Linda hadn't believed me when I told them that Señor Colón was on Isla Mujeres, and it was clear to me that no amount of protest would change their minds.

Obviously then, it was up to me to find out what he was doing out of jail and cruising around exotic resorts, free as a bird and cooking up more trouble. From what I knew of his past dealings, whatever he was up to was probably not only illegal, but also dangerous. Not to mention that it would only be a matter of time before he figured out my connection to Billy Joe. I was puzzling over what kind of partnership existed between Colón and Billy Joe as I was showering and brushing my hair, and thinking about Rudy, too. Ever since he'd met The Lovely Pamela, he'd become more smug and stuck-up towards me, always making references to my 'childish' behavior and contradicting everything I said. I knew it was probably only a Pamela-related phase he was going through but I couldn't help missing the old Rudy. I fell asleep vowing never to let something like love turn me into the kind of weirdo my brother had become.

Chapter Four

"I don't think we're all going to fit on it," Rudy remarked, watching the pier from the back seat of Julian's Chevy Suburban. We were in long line of cars awaiting the car ferry to Cancún. A man in dusty coveralls stepped forward in the early morning darkness and waved us ahead. Carefully, Julian moved the Chevy forward in line behind a semi truck.

"We'll all fit, you'll see," Julian replied. "The ferry is actually a lot bigger than it looks."

"Thanks again for driving," Linda told him from the back seat, tucking her fingers into Father's hand. "You're really going out of your way for us. I just hope we're not too much of an imposition."

"Not at all," Julian assured her cheerfully, inching forward to take a new place in the line, "it's a pleasure." I groaned and closed my eyes, trying to catch a few more minutes of sleep. Pleasure was not the word I would have used, not by a long shot. As far as I could see, the only good thing about leaving the island at that hour was the fact that we were leaving Señor Colón and his sinister, speedy henchman far behind.

At six-thirty in the morning Isla Mujeres is still dark and most people are still at home in bed, most sane people that is. Except for early-rising fishermen types, the island normally doesn't awake until around nine-thirty, which is about right as far as I'm concerned. Julian drove the Chevy up a metal ramp and parked it on the car ferry, edging it in beside a produce truck on one side and a Mazda pickup on the other side.

"Now what, Julian?" Rudy asked energetically. "Do we sit here in car the until we reach the mainland?"

"Only if you really want to. Otherwise you can come on up to the top deck and have a cup of coffee. You'll like it up there, the view is much better."

"K.C. fell asleep, she won't be going anywhere," Rudy commented with an air of superiority, and I opened my eyes just long enough to deny it.

"I'm wide awake," I told him, forcing back a yawn, "see?" Father shook his head in concern.

"Maybe you'd better stay here and sleep a little more, honey," he said kindly then murmured to Julian, "our K.C. is not really a morning person."

"I am too," I said and climbed out of the car, waving around at the rows of cars parked around us in the grey light of first dawn. "See? Me, morning girl, glad to be awake to greet the day." I gave them my best sarcastic smile as if to prove it and no one dared to contradict me.

"Well, coffee's this way," Julian informed us and led us to one side of the ferry where a long, narrow stairway led up two flights to an open air deck.

I followed along with everyone else, found a quiet seat on a bench and leaned against it, watching the waves below. The sea was a clear crystal green below us and even in the dim light I could see the coral reefs and dark beds of kelp growing right out of the water.

Father and Linda took seats across from me, and Rudy stood next to Julian near the small outdoor concession stand where two men were busy boiling water for instant coffee. My eyes drifted shut for a moment and then I forced them back open, standing up with a groan as I went to join Rudy and Julian.

I'm not usually a great fan of coffee but it does serve a purpose on occasion. The man with the hot water gave me a sympathetic smile and handed me a styrofoam cup. I added two heaping teaspoons of powdered coffee before Rudy could stop me.

"That stuff's really strong, K.C.," he warned me.

"I know what I'm doing, bro, I'm not a baby," I told him firmly, stirring the stuff thoroughly before taking my first sip. Jolt city! It tasted really nasty, far too strong for any amount of sugar to ever help. I drank it anyway because Rudy was watching but it didn't improve my mood at all.

"Is this your first trip to Mexico?" Julian asked, after a short silence during which I stirred the foul brew some more, hoping for the best.

"No. Father, Rudy and I went to Puerto Vallarta a few months back. I like Mexico a lot." I took another sip but then wished I hadn't. The man at the concession stand caught my eye and waved happily, inviting me back for seconds. I smiled and waved back weakly, hoisting my cup with an enthusiasm I definitely didn't feel.

"I think you'll enjoy seeing the ruins of Chichén Itzá," Julian told me soothingly as Father and Linda wandered over to join us. Predictably, they had their arms around each other and they both looked wide awake and vibrant. I sighed.

"What does 'Chichén Itzá' mean, anyway?" Rudy asked Julian as the ferry pulled into the dock of Punta Sam and we all headed back downstairs to the Chevy. Unnoticed, I dropped the rest of my coffee into a trash can before I climbed into the vehicle. Julian started the engine.

"Chi means water, chén means mouth and Itzá is the name of the first people who lived where the city was later built," Julian told us, pulling off the ferry into light morning traffic. "You have to keep in mind that the Yucatán Peninsula is almost entirely composed of limestone and sandstone; and there are virtually no aboveground rivers or streams, only underwater rivers and sink hole wells. The sacred well at Chichén Itzá was believed to have been the home of Chac, God of Rain."

"Isn't he the one they made all those sacrifices to?" Linda asked, scribbling in her notebook.

"Yes, the Mayans believed that they could bring rain and therefore fertility to the land by offering sacrifices to Chac."

"Human sacrifices, right?" Rudy shivered.

"That's right. At first, the ancient Mayans used to offer small animals, children and young men as gifts to Chac. Later, as they developed a more warlike culture, they sacrificed their prisoners of war to Chac, instead of killing off their own relatives and friends."

"Pretty barbaric," Father commented dryly.

Julian shrugged and continued, "They were a deeply religious people. Their beliefs demanded that they sacrifice no less than the best they had to offer if they wanted rain for their crops." There was silence in the car for a while as we all pondered this.

"Aren't they the ones with the ball game? The game where they combined sports with a religious ceremony?"

I asked. Julian gave me an interested glance in the rear view mirror.

"That's right, K.C. The game was called *pok-ta-pok*. It was a little like basketball, but played with a football-shaped stone, and the hoops were vertical instead of horizontal. The game ended once one team scored one goal by getting the 'ball' through the opposing team's hoop. They could only make contact with the 'ball' using their hips, knees and elbows." At the mention of sports Rudy perked right up.

"Like weird soccer or something." Here, my older brother pantomimed knocking a ball through a hoop with his elbow, nearly smacking me in the side of the head in his enthusiasm. "He shoots! He scores!"

"Hey, watch it," I grumbled, ducking. Julian shook his head.

"But that was only part of it," he added dryly. "Remember, it was a religious ceremony as well. The captain of the losing team was ritually beheaded, his blood was spilled as an offering to the gods and, if he wished it, the captain of the winning team was allowed the privilege of offering himself for beheading as well."

"Um, privilege?" Rudy gulped and hugged his elbows to his sides defensively, clearly appalled by this ghastly 'reward' for success.

"The Mayas had a very different perspective on life and death," Julian explained.

"I should say so," Rudy muttered.

"But not everything they did was about sacrifice," Linda put in quickly. "They were great mathematicians and astronomers too. Their calendar is almost as accurate as ours, and dates back thousands of years."

"That's right," Julian agreed, "some say the Mayas were the first people to use the concept of 'zero' in a numerical system. They were also the first people of Mesoamerica to develop their own system of writing.

"Their alphabet is completely original and consists of letter-drawings known as 'pictograms.' They were artists, philosophers and warriors all rolled into one."

"Where did they go?" Father wanted to know. "What happened to the Mayan culture?"

"The Spaniards wiped out most of them. In the mid-1500's a Franciscan priest by the name of Diego Landa came to the Yucatán and made it his mission to convert the Mayans. He did this by destroying thousands of Mayan idols, and by burning their books."

"They burned books?" I was shocked. "Why would the Spanish want to destroy the Mayan culture?" Julian shot me an amused glance in the mirror.

"Well, as far as book-burning goes, did you ever learn about the Spanish Inquisition in school? For the rest, let's just say the Spaniards were appalled by the Maya's religious practices."

"But it's not like the Spaniards were upstanding citizens either," I argued. "After all, *they* were the ones who invaded and then destroyed the Mayan cicilization for little or no reason. I mean, they came to the Yucatán in search of slaves, right? How ethical was that?"

Julian sighed. "It's all a matter of cultural context, isn't it, and of who won?" There was a long silence in the car after his words as we all pondered the vagaries of mankind.

The drive to Chichén Itzá took us west for nearly three hours along Mexico Highway 180. We passed through many small towns, just clusters of houses with thatched roofs, stick walls and dirt floors. I didn't see any telephone or electric wires attached to these dwellings and was amazed at the difference between my own standard of living and that of the people of the Yucatán.

"The remaining Mayas still live in this region much the way they always have," Julian explained. "They publish newspapers and magazines in their own language, despite the fact that Spanish is now the official language of Mexico."

"Good for them," I muttered, still incensed by the Spanish Conquistadors' near-destruction of the Mayan culture.

We slowed for one of the wicked speed bumps in the road which mark the city limits of each town and a small boy approached the window, selling a cluster of small green fruit pods for a few pesos. I rolled down the window and gave him twenty for the entire bunch. After washing off the fruit with some bottled water, I shared it around. It was tangy, sweet, and refreshing.

"They call it *guaya*," Julian told me with a smile, forestalling my question. "It comes from an evergreen tree, if you can believe it, and grows all over the Yucatán."

We pulled into the parking lot of the Chichén Itzá National Institute of Anthropology and History, and I climbed out, glad to stretch my legs after the long road trip. Julian left the Chevy parked in the shade of two enormous palm trees and we headed for the museum entrance where, for 45 pesos, we obtained admission to the museum and to the ruins themselves.

"What do you think?" Julian smiled at us. "Museum first, or ruins?"

"Ruins."

"Ruins." Rudy and I spoke simultaneously in a moment of rare total agreement with each other. Linda nodded vigorously, pulling her camera from its bag.

"Ruins it is then," Father said. We headed past the museum and into the bright, hot sun.

Kukulcán's pyramid was the first thing I saw, looming impressively. It must have been almost three hundred feet tall if it was an inch. I stopped dead in my tracks and gazed up at it in awe. Rudy looked back over his shoulder at me standing there as he headed for the carved stone steps leading up one side of the pyramid.

"Come on K.C., last one up has to do a double dare!" He threatened me with our old childhood game, but I still stood there, staring upward. "What's the matter, are you scared?" He smirked condescendingly at me and I shook my head with bravado I didn't quite feel inside.

"Of course I'm not scared," I replied, following him up the face of the pyramid.

Each step was about seven inches deep and a foot tall. Either the Mayas had had very small feet, or they'd built the steps steeply like that to deter attackers. Or perhaps both. About halfway up the pyramid I made the mistake of looking down and my breath caught in my throat.

There were no handrails and the stone was crumbling slightly so when I reached the top I stayed back from the very edge. I was looking out over the ruins from a height which rendered the trees below dwarf-like. Linda and Father then reached the top too, and we all stood there gaping at the magnificence of Mayan architecture.

Chapter Five

"More than a thousand years and it's still standing," Linda breathed.

"They could teach us a thing or two about building to last," Father agreed. He's a lawyer for an international construction company; he knows a lot about building to last and he's not an easy man to impress.

"There are four sides to the pyramid," Julian pointed and we followed his gaze, "ninety-one steps leading up to the top on each of the sides adds up to three hundred and sixty four, plus the sanctuary behind us (I turned to look at the square building at my back) is one more, which makes three hundred and sixty five, the number of days in a year.

"Each side of the pyramid has fifty two panels," Julian went on, "which is the number of years in a cycle, and each side of the nine terraces leading up are divided by stairs into eighteen sections, because they had eighteen months in their calendar." Rudy whistled under his breath.

"So this thing is like a gigantic clock?" Julian nodded.

"In a way. And there's more." We all listened intently as he continued his little lecture. "The pyramid is constructed in such a way that every year, on the vernal equinox and autumnal equinox at about three o'clock in the afternoon, the shadows cast by the terraced faces form another shadow which resembles a snake creeping downward on the stairs until it joins the serpent's head carved in stone at the bottom. A lot of people come every year to watch it. The snake represents Kukulcán, the feathered serpent, also known as Quetzlcoatl."

"Huh," I murmured in awe. "So the Mayas not only knew all about the equinoxes but were able to actually build a pyramid to commemorate them?"

"The equinoxes corresponded with some of the rituals they celebrated at the beginning of the agricultural cycles of the year."

"Cool." I was at a loss for words. Julian walked around the stone building at the top, pointing out the rest of the ruins below us.

"Over there is the ball court, and you can see the temple of the Jaguars from here. It's that big blocky building on the end there. That's where the high priests sat during the games."

"Yeah, probably sharpening their knives the whole time," Rudy muttered resentfully. I could tell that he still wasn't exactly comfortable with the fate of the players of the ball game. In his world, winning the big game means a victory celebration, then sweet promotional deals and maybe even a tour. What it definitely does *not* include is the beheading of the players.

"And you can see the Temples of the North and South from here — there's one at each end there, see?" I leaned forward for a better look and Julian put a steadying hand on my shoulder.

"Careful, K.C."

"I'm fine, but thanks."

Father and Linda had walked around to the other side of the sanctuary and we followed them. Inside the sanctuary was little more than a stone floor and a few, eroded carvings. It had a certain very feeling though, and I avoided going inside more from instinct than from any reason.

"What's that?" Linda pointed at a square structure about two hundred yards distant, looming upwards from amid a forest of stone pillars.

"That's the Temple of the Warriors and all around it is the Group of the Thousand Columns. The columns were used to support a large roof, probably made of thatch like houses here have today." I looked down at the tall stone pillars where they stood like bones bleached white by the sun and I shivered, in spite of the heat.

There was something peculiar about looking at the skeletal remains of a civilization which had been at its height over a thousand years ago. It was kind of "here today, gone tomorrow," and I felt as though my own life were nothing compared to the cycles of time which had elapsed since this great city had been strong.

"Ready to go down now, kids?" Father asked suddenly.

"Sure," I nodded confidently, before I looked over the edge. While the stairs had seemed steep on the way up, they seemed vertical when I looked down and the nausea hit.

"Are you afraid of heights?" said Julian, who had lingered behind the others, watching me. I shook my head.

"I'm usually not. Well, maybe a little right now," I admitted reluctantly, since Rudy was too far away to hear.

"It's OK, you'll be fine if you go slowly," Julian told me reassuringly, putting his arm around my shoulders, "it often affects people this way." With Julian guiding me firmly but gently down, I relaxed after taking a few steps, but was still glad to reach the ground again.

"Can we take a closer look at the pillars over there?" Linda asked and Julian nodded.

"Sure, why not." We crossed the baked grass toward the Temple of the Warriors and I was intrigued by a wooden door which was built into the side of a stairway leading to the top of the temple.

"Where does that go?" I asked Julian.

"There are chambers inside the Temples."

"Can we go in?" I asked eagerly but he shook his head regretfully.

"Sorry, but all that's off limits to tourists." I frowned, unreasonably disappointed as he continued: "Many of the ruins are in such a state of decay that they're not only inaccessible, but downright dangerous."

I would have climbed to the top of the Temple of the Warriors itself to examine the reclining god figure of a *chac mool* on the top but there was a yellow nylon cord blocking the stairs. Apparently the Mexican Government didn't want tourists to injure themselves on the crumbling steps of the ruins.

We wandered around the city of Chichén Itzá for the better part of an hour, exploring the buildings as best we could from the outside.

"What's up with all the carvings?" Rudy pointed to the elaborate stone walls, on which were carved figures of plants and animals and other odd shapes.

"I don't know what all of them mean," Julian admitted. "Some of them obviously represent the various Mayan deities and some of them tell stories about the daily life associated with these places but the majority of the symbols are still a mystery. I've applied for a grant to study them further, as a matter of fact." Rudy nodded and gave the carvings a few more seconds of contemplation before strolling off to join Father and Linda. I lingered behind with Julian.

"That one looks like a tic-tac-toe board," I remarked, pointing to a square design which covered an entire section of the wall before us. It was a pattern I recognized from the cobbled streets of the towns we'd passed through, and I pointed it out to Julian.

"You'll see a lot of these ancient designs in modern Mayan art, blanket designs, pottery, embroidery," he replied, "it's all still here."

Father, Rudy and Linda were waiting for us to catch up to them, and when we did Father suggested a break for lunch. I could tell it was Rudy's idea because he gets a certain grim look about the eyes when he's hungry.

"There's a restaurant not far from here, it's convenient and the food is not half bad," Julian told us as he consulted his map. "Otherwise we could drive a few miles to Valladolid and look for another place." We opted for the restaurant with the practically unpronounceable name of Xaybe'h, close to the ruins, so that we could resume our exploration after lunch.

The restaurant was made of pink stucco and featured a courtyard surrounding a pool beside which other diners were having lunch. I soon settled gratefully into my chair and attacked a heaping plate of delicious Aztec pie (made of corn tortillas and tomato sauce with cheese, kind of a Mexican Shepherd's pie). For a long time no one spoke.

"That's better," Rudy pushed his plate back and tilted his chair dangerously back on two legs, apparently feeling more like his usual self. "So how about those wacky Mayas?" It was a rhetorical remark and we treated it as such, finishing our food with smiles. Rudy leaned forward, bringing his chair down with a thump. "Why don't we go back and explore the ruins some more, that is if it's not too much of a sacrifice. Get it? *Sacrifice?*" The others regarded Rudy patiently and I rolled my eyes at his corny joke.

"Ha ha, very funny, Rudy."

"Well it was," he returned, mildly irritated.

"Are we ready?" Father pushed back his chair and stood up, saying, "I think I'd like to use the washroom before we get underway again."

"Good idea," Linda agreed, joining him. "Just give us a few minutes and we'll be ready to go, Rudy." I left the table and strolled along the poolside, enjoying the cool breeze which stirred the summer air. Stopping in the shadow of a souvenir stand to buy postcards, I happened to glance up as a white sedan pulled into the parking lot of the restaurant and I watched as a man climbed out from the driver's side of the car.

Something about the way he moved chilled my heart and then I recognized the man who had chased me the day before on Isla Mujeres. He hadn't seen me yet so I whirled and headed for the sanctuary of the restaurant, moving so quickly that I smacked into Julian who was on his way out.

"Hey K.C., what's up?" Julian steadied me, his eyes concerned. "You OK?" I shook my head and glanced over my shoulder.

"There's this guy out there, the same one who chased me yesterday!" I whispered.

"What's this all about, now?" Julian was taken aback and I took advantage of his confusion to push past him inside the restaurant, hoping that my pursuer hadn't seen us. Julian followed me, nonplussed. "Who's chasing you, K.C.?" I peered over his shoulder apprehensively, there was no sign of the man, but that didn't make me feel better since it meant he could be anywhere.

I explained briefly to Julian: "A few months ago I helped the police in Puerto Vallarta catch this corrupt politician, Hernán Colón." Julian's eyes narrowed as I continued breathlessly, "Anyway, I saw him on Isla Mujeres yesterday, but what's worse, he saw *me* and his friend chased me until I lost him. He must be following me, we have to tell the police!" Julian's eyes narrowed at my words and he shook his head slowly.

"You helped catch Señor Colón?" he repeated slowly. "I do remember reading about him, but surely you're mistaken about him being on Isla Mujeres, he's in jail now," he told me firmly. Equally firmly I shook my head at him.

"Oh no he's not, Julian! I tell you he's after me!" I realized that my words sounded slightly hysterical and took a few unsteady breaths to calm myself.

"Who's after you?" Father, Linda and Rudy joined us then.

"The same guy who chased me yesterday!" I repeated for their benefit. "I just saw him, he's out there right now!" Father and Linda exchanged worried glances and Linda shook her head.

"Calm down, K.C. honey," she told me soothingly, "no one is after you. You're safe here with us."

"Get a grip, Kook Case," Rudy added, getting in his two cents worth as he shook his head at Julian and made a circle around his temple with his finger. "Don't mind K.C., she just sees things like this sometimes."

"I do not 'see' things!" I was suddenly furious with all of them. "I don't see why you won't believe me, I'm telling you he's right outside, look, I'll show you!" I pushed boldly past them into the bright sunlight, intending to point out the white sedan. To my mingled distress and relief, the car was gone. Father, Linda and Julian watched as I shook my head slowly, repeating,

"Well, he was here just a moment ago. I know that." Father draped a comforting arm across my shoulders, obviously worried.

"K.C., calm down. Señor Colón is in jail, and there's no one following you."

"You're really losing it." Rudy added with typical generosity.

"I am not losing it!" I snapped, "I know what I saw!"

"K.C., nobody thinks you're crazy," Father put in quickly, frowning hard at Rudy. "It's just that you're having a hard time letting go of your trauma from Puerto Vallarta, it's made you overly afraid and inclined to misinterpret things."

"Fine," I muttered, realizing that to say anything more would only make matters worse and I might even end up in a straightjacket. I resolved to keep my mouth shut about Señor Colón from then on since no one would believe me anyway. Needless to say, we were all very quiet as we got back into the Chevy.

After lunch, we explored the southern section of the ruins, known as old Chichén Itzá, where some of the most ancient buildings in the complex were located. Julian took us around the Nunnery, where the High Priestesses had lived, after which we trekked down a long dusty road to the Ossuary, where the Mayan officials were buried. After that we hiked around to the Deer House, about which Julian was unable to tell us much other than that it was called that because carvings of deer were once found on its outside walls.

"I don't see any deer there now," Rudy grumbled. "Pretty silly to call a building a 'deer' house when you can't even see any deer."

I could tell that my older brother was beginning to get tired of exploring. His face had taken on the look of yearning which I had come to associate with thoughts of The Lovely Pamela and sure enough, we hadn't taken two more steps before he was rhapsodizing on about her.

It turns out that Pamela is quite possibly the only living, breathing incarnation of perfection in the twentieth century; her beauty is only equaled by her intelligence and wit, which are apparently boundless. She made all other women seem pale by comparison, including Mayas, ancient or not. I was momentarily distracted from constantly scanning the ruins around me for villainous strangers by Rudy's remarks.

"Yeah, you're right," I observed, "big noses and crossed eyes were considered a form of beauty by the ancient Mayas. Pamela would fit right in." Linda threw a reproachful look at me.

"K.C.," she began and I added innocently:

"Well it's true, they did," I was referring to the ancient Mayan custom of dangling beads in front of the eyes of newborn babes to induce slightly cross-eyed look.

"What's that building over there? Rudy, could you hand me the guide book?" Linda pointed hastily to a structure in the distance, hoping to distract Rudy. It didn't work.

"Shut up, K.C., you just dislike Pamela because she's so pretty and you're so, well —" Rudy's words trailed off and he swept a disparaging glance over me — "you probably just wish you could be more like her," he finished with a shrug, handing Linda her guide book.

"You're right," I answered smoothly, "and I think I'll start with a lobotomy." Rudy scowled darkly at me and opened his mouth to speak, but Father held up his hand.

"Enough," he said, and although it was just one word it carried the weight of dozens. We shut up.

After that I deliberately lagged behind the others as Julian led them toward the Temple of the Initial Series, the building near which he and Beau and Billy Joe had made their famous discovery. The actual find, a stone tablet representing August 13, 3114 B.C., the beginning of the Mayan calendar (or 'long count' as it was known in scholarly circles), was in the National Museum.

"Just a little to the left," Linda directed Julian, posing him in front of the ruins which had catapulted him to fame. Julian looked mildly uncomfortable with the process, but tolerated it patiently. "That's great!" Linda enthused. "This is going to make a terrific story, Julian, thanks."

"It's OK," he flashed her an amused grin. "I really don't mind. It's nice to get away from Isla Mujeres for a while. Besides, it's good publicity. Who knows? Maybe someone will read your article and decide to donate money for more excavation and reconstruction."

"You mean there's more to be uncovered?" My mind boggled at the idea.

"There are a lot more sites around here which have yet to be excavated. It's a shame but there simply isn't enough money to finance the undertaking." Julian's face assumed a far-off look, as though he were envisioning the day when he would be able to complete the excavation of Chichén Itzá.

I decided my future on the spot and told Julian, "I'll definitely get my degree in archaeology and come help you." Rudy laughed rudely.

"You'd be better off majoring in 'Pest-ology'. They'd probably even give you an honorary degree." I glowered at my brother, fully intending to put him in his place but before I could do so Father swiftly changed the subject.

"There's plenty of time for both of you kids to decide what you want to do with your lives. Keep up your grades and who knows? The sky's the limit."

Rudy and I stared blankly at each other, then looked away, somehow disarmed by Father's tangential remark. I think we were both amazed by how he managed to work the topic of keeping up grades into our dispute. At any rate, we stopped fighting for a while.

Chapter Six

We walked slowly back toward the north zone of
Chichén Itzá. The air was almost milky in the heat.
Around me, insects buzzed and chattered, and I could
hear strange bird songs coming from the woods. When we
returned to the National Institute of Anthropology and
History, Linda expressed a desire to check out the small
museum store.

"You coming too, K.C.?" she asked, when I lingered
behind.

"No, but do me a favor, OK? If you see a bumper
sticker or pin saying 'I left my heart in Chichén Itzá,' get
it for me would you?" Linda grinned.

"Sure."

I decided to wait outside and stopped to adjust my
sandals in the shade of a big leafy tree with some kind of
weird airplane plant growing from the bark about halfway
up its trunk. The sandal strap had worked itself under my
heel and I frowned, tightening it. The last thing I needed
in the tropical climate was a blister on my foot. I had a
perfect view of the pyramid and was tired enough to take
a break so I rested in the shade for a while longer, jotting
notes in my notebook and snapping a few pictures for the
record. I studied the pyramid, keeping a wary eye out for

white sedans and suspicious-looking guys heading toward me while thinking of the people who had lived here in the time of Chichén Itzá's grandest era. I closed my eyes. From high atop Kukulcán's pyramid I could imagine the open plains spreading out, rolling endlessly toward the horizon. Thatched-roof houses and crude stucco shanties crowded the fields around the pyramid, forming a city that sprawled in all directions. The pyramid was not the bland colored stone of today, but was richly stained in vibrant reds, yellows and greens.

Men ran nimbly up and down the pyramid steps, and the very top was busy with guards protecting the sanctuary and the dignitaries who worked within the structure. From the top of the pyramid, all of the buildings in the complex would be visible, distant mounds of color amid a vast city of low houses.

The ball court would be alive with voices, the cheers of the crowd and the shouts of the players mingling as a player hurled himself across the huge court at a run. Twisting and diving through the opposing players, he'd leap from the carved, slanted panel at the bottom of the playing wall, slamming himself up and against the stone wall close to where the ring hung. He would only have a split second to bat the ball with all his might through the ring. Playing for keeps.

I shivered at the thought of the priests waiting patiently for the outcome of the game. And how it would have felt to have been the captain of the losing team, to walk up those steps, knowing that certain death lay ahead. I heard approaching footsteps and opened my eyes to smile at Julian as he appeared from inside the museum.

"Hey K.C., what's up?" Julian joined me, sinking to the grass and leaning against the back of the tree as I was doing.

"I was tired, so I took a break," I explained simply. "Say, Julian? I just wanted to say, well you know, thanks for showing us around like this when you probably have better things to do with your time." He gave me a considering look then shrugged, smiling a little.

"It's been a pleasure, K.C. I like showing people around this place. The Mayas had a truly great civilization that just doesn't get the kind of recognition it deserves."

"Might have something to do with that custom they had of carving the beating hearts out of their victims," I commented mildly. "That sort of thing tends to put people off a bit." Julian grinned at me.

"Yeah, that might have something to do with it." Father, Linda and Rudy joined us then and unanimously we decided to call it a day, as far as exploring was concerned. On the way back Julian suggested that we stop at an underground cave called Dzitnup where the water was cold, clear and fresh enough for swimming.

We needed no persuasion other than the word 'swim', so Julian turned off highway 180 about four kilometers from the town of Valladolid. We parked in a small lot with a few other cars, where locals were selling postcards and quartz figurines to tourists.

Behind some trees was a narrow, damp limestone pathway leading straight down into the earth. For a few pesos, an old man in a blue and yellow striped lawn chair at the entrance permitted us to descend.

The steps were twisted and steep, and I clung to the knotted rope which served as a handrail. About halfway down I had to stoop to avoid bumping my head on the ceiling of the tunnel.

Farther along, the pathway widened out into a huge underground chamber. I straightened up and looked around, as awed by the natural beauty of the place as I had been by Chichén Itzá's man-made splendor.

A small hole at the top of the cave permitted light to illuminate the entire area. I gazed down at a clear crystal green pool over which hung calcified tree roots, enormous stalactites nearly reaching down to the surface of the water.

"Go ahead," Julian told me, "it's great for cooling off." I slid out of my clothes, glad that all those hours of wearing my bathing suit underneath were about to pay off. The water was cold, obviously fed from an underground stream and I floated blissfully in the water, looking up at the blue sky through the small cave-top opening.

Linda paddled by and I watched approvingly as she splashed Father playfully then dove under the clear water when he retaliated in kind. Rudy floated off by himself, looking up at the stalactites with a dreamy look on his face, and I knew he was thinking of The Lovely Pamela.

An unsettling idea occurred to me as I floated there and I swam across the cave toward Julian. He was reclining on one of the smooth sandstone boulders at the edge of the pool, half in and half out of the water.

"Say Julian?"

"What's up, K.C.?"

"This wouldn't be a *sacred* well, now would it?" I asked, very casually. He looked at me thoughtfully.

"Probably was once, why?" I licked my lips and looked nervously beneath the water at the white sand clearly visible at the bottom of the cave.

"Well, it wouldn't be one of those sacred *sacrificial* wells, would it?" I was thinking of the well at Chichén Itzá, where living people had been ritually flung to their deaths, offerings to the Rain God Chac. Julian smiled.

"I don't think so, but maybe." The thought made me feel distinctly uneasy and I paddled around for a little while longer before climbing up the smooth limestone rocks and out of the water. I studied the cave for a long time, wondering what lay beneath the white sand floor of the pool then decided it was ancient history anyway and went back in for another swim.

The trip home was uneventful except for when we slowed for a speed bump and I looked out the window to find myself face to face with four grubby little boys clutching what looked like a large orange rat. Julian stopped the car.

"Fifty pesos, señorita," one of them said, thrusting the poor creature against the glass of the side-door window which I rolled down for a better look. Whatever it was, the creature looked almost lifeless. A thick cotton string had been wound tightly around its neck and its eyes were glazed. I could see it panting desperately in the hot sun.

"I'll take it," I said firmly, pushing a hundred-peso note at the little boy holding the creature. After one amazed look at the bill he handed over the animal, which lay limply in my hands as though dead.

"K.C.!" Father protested, "what on earth do you think you're doing?" I clutched the creature defensively, working to untie the cord which was strangling it. It opened its eyes briefly them closed them again, clearly resigned to its fate at my hands.

"It looks like it needs water," I explained feebly, already wondering if I'd done the right thing. "I couldn't just let it die." Linda came to my rescue.

"It does look pretty weak, James. It probably wouldn't have lasted for much longer like that." I gave her a grateful look as Rudy muttered:

"Kook Case." I ignored him and finished untying the creature. To my relief it lay quietly in my lap, exhausted.

"It's a kind of native raccoon called a kinkajou," Julian explained with some amusement. "They're sometimes kept as pets around here. This one is just a baby." I looked down at it with interest.

"A kinkajou, huh?" Where I come from raccoons are brown with white ringed faces, this one was orange like a fox and had a long striped tail. "It doesn't look much like a raccoon."

"See K.C. go on a trip. See K.C. buy a rabid animal which bites her and gives her fleas and rabies. Go, K.C., go." Rudy mocked my altruism and I glared at him as I cuddled the small creature.

"It's tame, it won't bite, and it doesn't have fleas or rabies anyway." I informed him coldly.

"How do you know?" he asked, always the stickler for details.

"I can just *tell*," I answered and he threw up his hands in disgust.

"All right, but when we're taking you to the hospital I'm going to be saying 'I told you so' the whole way there," he sounded a little too pleased with this image.

"Shut up, Rudy," I muttered, unscrewing the cap of my water bottle. I poured a lid full of water for the kinkajou and in seconds it had finished that so I poured another capful. The kinkajou stopped drinking after four capfuls then burrowed softly into my lap. Within minutes it was asleep. When I glanced up I was surprised to find myself the recipient of Father's, Linda's and Rudy's speculative stares. They were just looking strangely at me, all except for Julian who was driving.

"What?" I asked, a little defensively. Father cleared his throat.

"So, K.C., would you care to enlighten us as to your plans for the kinkajou?" His tone was dry. "You do realize, of course, that customs officers frown on people who try to bring live animals across international borders?" I looked at him blankly.

"Um —" I began, momentarily at a loss.

"It's all right, I'll take care of the kinkajou for you when you leave, if you like," Julian offered. "They're very intelligent and make great pets." I smiled at him brilliantly.

"You're sure you don't mind?"

He shook his head, saying, "A friend of mind on Isla Mujeres has a full-grown kinkajou. I've always thought it would be fun to have one." Father heaved a huge sigh of relief from the back seat and Linda chuckled.

"Got your shots?" Rudy asked him caustically and Julian smiled good-naturedly.

"I doubt this one would bite, it seems pretty tame, but I'll have the local vet take a look at it just the same."

"What are you going to call it, K.C.?" Linda wanted to know and I pursed my lips thoughtfully.

"Kook Case Junior," Rudy persisted, trying to annoy me and I gave him a warning look. He was really starting to get on my nerves.

"Shut up, Rudy. I'm calling her *Topés*," I told Linda, it was the Spanish word for the speed bump which had stopped us. Rudy blew out his cheeks and crossed his eyes at me but I ignored him. Even if it *was* a little unusual for me to buy a pet by the road side, Rudy didn't have to be so mean about it. I resolved never to speak to him again for the rest of my life. Or longer!

The kinkajou stirred, shifted around then went back to sleep in my lap, where it remained for the duration of the trip back to Isla Mujeres.

When we reached the apartment my first order of business was to find a small cardboard box for Topés, then food and water dishes. Fortunately the kitchen was equipped and I was able to make use of a saucer, a bowl and some leftover pieces of fish from the refrigerator for my new friend.

Topés was asleep in the box by the time I got back with her food but she woke up when I put the bowls of food and water in there with her and wasted no time devouring much of what I'd brought her.

"Wow, you were hungry," I remarked.

"Still am," Rudy grouched from the sofa.

"I was talking to Topés," I told him frostily.

"Oh," Rudy shrugged disinterestedly and went back to the fascinating spectacle of women in bikinis balancing atop water skis, his admiration for their talent apparent from the way he was drooling at them.

I left the apartment and looked out from the rooftop toward the north beach where the yacht had been docked the day before. There was no sign of it anywhere, the pier was deserted. Apparently Señor Colón had packed up and left the island. Feeling greatly relieved I headed downstairs to the lobby.

Typical of the rest of the hotel, it featured an airy patio decorated with lush green hanging plants and small wrought iron tables at which people sat, sipping cool drinks and listening to the party music coming from a visiting cruise ship at the pier. I found a deserted table behind a giant potted palm and sat down to relax in the shade with a tall, frosty glass of lemonade.

That's how I came to see Billy Joe for the first time since dinner the night before. He was sitting at a small table towards the front of the lobby and I could see him well enough to notice the small piece of bloodstained tissue still stuck to his face from a nasty shaving wound.

As I watched, Billy Joe took a long drag of his cigarette, stubbed it out then lit another one, his eyes shifting restlessly up and down the street as though he were waiting for someone.

He looked nervous and tired, there were dark shadows under his eyes and his lips moved now and then as though he were muttering angrily to himself. As I watched he lit another cigarette, despite the fact that he already had one going, and took a long puff from it as Beau joined him, from inside the hotel.

Now I would (of course!) never deliberately eavesdrop on a conversation which is not meant for me, but the way I see it, when people are talking in public they should expect that others might be listening. And if I happened to overhear something of interest, well there you are, pure happenstance. I leaned forward slightly.

"Took you long enough," Billy Joe said sourly.

"Ran into Julian," Beau replied blandly, helping himself to a cigarette from Billy Joe's pack, "back from his day with Ms. Hébert and company." There was so much noise from the street, I could barely make out what the two of them were saying.

"What's up with that, anyway?" Billy Joe grunted. "The last thing we need is some nosy reporter snooping around the site." At this point a gaily-painted ice cream truck rounded the corner, piping out a tinkling melody which drowned out the rest of his words. Frustrated, I could only wait until it had passed, while watching as Beau and Billy talked to each other intently.

"... the Boss?" Billy Joe's cigarette had burned down to a stub but he inhaled it anyway. "What did he want?"

"He wants results, and soon," Beau replied grimly. "Said we have to finish in three days, tops. Boss says some nosy kid has been snooping around, making trouble for him. Thinks the kid may have tipped off the police, or something. He had to leave the island before the kid could put the finger on him."

"Kid?" Billy Joe shook his head, "what kid?"

"Some tourist brat or something, he didn't say." Beau took a long drag from his cigarette and added, "Anyway, we have to wrap things up."

"No way," Billy Joe said flatly, "we just finished setting up, it's gonna take time."

"Then we're going to have to start working at night," Beau remarked. Billy Joe just shook his head, flicking his cigarette into the street where it smoldered forlornly on the cobblestones.

"No way we're going be able to pull off two shifts," he repeated, scowling. "It's way too risky." Beau ran a hand through his hair, nervously slicking it back and hunched his shoulders.

"We have to. Anyway at night it'll be easier, and less crowded."

Now, as you might imagine I was finding this conversation exceedingly strange, not to mention more than a little alarming. I mean, restoring the Temple of Ixchel was obviously necessary. The way things were, a person could walk right past the ruins and almost mistake them for a big pile of rocks. But I couldn't see why the restoration would be so urgent as to prompt a round-the-clock effort on the part of Julian and his crew.

The fact that the "Boss" had warned Billy Joe and Beau about a "nosy kid" was enough to confirm my suspicions that Señor Colón was the man they were working for and despite fearing for my own personal safety I couldn't help wondering what it was that Colón had to hide. Even more puzzling was the question of how Billy Joe and Beau were involved. It was only a matter of time before they figured out who the "nosy kid" was, and then I would really be in trouble since the two of them could lead Señor Colón straight to me.

Chapter Seven

"There you are, K.C., I've been looking all over for you," Linda called to me cheerily from a few feet away and I straightened up abruptly, assuming the look of someone who had definitely not been eavesdropping on others. "You ready for dinner?" I quickly crossed the lobby to her side so she wouldn't have to shout.

"Sure," I said and followed her into the restaurant, hoping that Beau and Billy Joe hadn't heard us.

Father and Rudy were waiting for us at our usual table, the one near the balcony with a view of the small harbor. We ordered the evening special, and I helped myself to a side dish of everything I could tuck into a napkin for Topés.

"How did you like the ruins today?" Father asked us conversationally, and I grinned at him.

"They were great, let's go back again tomorrow." I was only joking, but Rudy took me seriously.

"Count me out, Kook Case," he stated sourly. "I'm going snorkeling tomorrow." Father and Linda exchanged that look which adults use, the one they think kids don't notice.

"Didn't you have a good time today?" Linda asked my brother carefully.

"Yeah, I guess," Rudy pushed a slice of smoked fish around on his plate unenthusiastically. "It was cool, in a way."

"Cool, in a way?!" I was so disgusted by Rudy's underwhelming description of Chichén Itzá that I forgot my resolve never to speak to him again. "Come on, admit it, it was way better than anything you've ever seen before!" Rudy shrugged and chewed for a moment before replying.

"I guess." Father and Linda gave each other the 'look' again.

"Is there something bothering you, Rudy?" Father asked my older brother. "You seem a little ... on edge lately," he finished tactfully. I was glad to know that I wasn't the only one who had noticed Rudy's crankiness.

"It's that old 'Pamela' hex again," I informed Father and Linda sarcastlically. "I already told you he's going through *witch*drawal."

"Shut up, K.C." Rudy scowled at me, flushing under his tan, "I am not. I'm just, I don't know, bored with kid stuff."

"Kid stuff?" I began indignantly and Father cut me off.

"Look, Rudy, I know it's hard for you to be away from Pamela," he began and shot me a hard glance when I choked on my Pepsi, "but it's only for a week, and believe me, the time will fly by." Rudy sighed.

"You don't understand," he told us, his eyes getting that far-off look I had come to dread. "This is different, she's special. She's beautiful, and popular, and I really like her." I took advantage of the fact that everyone was watching Rudy to put a handful of fresh cherries for Topés in my shirt pocket.

"Pamela is a very nice girl and I can see why you like her," Father replied, "but you have to remember to live in the present. Moping your vacation away won't help anything and you'll miss out on a lot of fun while you're here." Rudy stared at his plate and shrugged.

"Sure," he said without enthusiasm. And that was the end of that.

Sometimes I feel sorry for parents. They try so hard to give us the benefit of their experience but the thing adults forget is that sometimes you have to try things for yourself before you realize they were right all along.

Anyway, I could have told Father that his lecture wouldn't work, I'd been trying to reason with my big brother ever since the day he'd met Pamela for the first time at a cheerleading rally and decided then and there that she was the girl he intended to marry.

"Why don't you call her?" Linda suggested after a moment's reflection and Rudy gazed at her, hope dawning in his eyes.

"You mean tonight? From here?"

"Sure, why not?" Linda replied. "It'll be a little expensive but worth it if you'll feel better. Remember that time you called me from the Philippines, James?" Rudy and I watched with deep interest as my Father actually blushed.

"Don't go and bore the kids with that story," he mumbled but Linda grinned at us and leaned forward, ignoring his protest.

"It was the sweetest thing, your Father called me at three in the morning to tell me he loved me."

"You did that?" Rudy was intrigued, "at three in the morning?"

78

"I forgot about the time difference," Father explained weakly. This was a part of him he doesn't often share with his children, the soft, white underbelly of his Irish romantic side.

"I almost hung up on him, I thought it was an obscene phone call because the operator didn't speak any English or French and kept repeating 'are you there' with this weird accent." Linda chuckled, remembering. "It was so romantic." She got slightly misty as she and Father shared a special smile.

"Excuse me, please." Rudy got up and left the table, with something of his old energy evident in the way he almost sprinted for the reception desk. I sighed and shook my head, once again resolving never to fall in love. I mean, look at all the weird stuff it makes people do.

"Hello there," Julian said from right behind me. "Mind if I join you?"

"Please do," I beamed up at him and scooted my chair over quickly so that he could sit next to me at Rudy's empty spot. Unfortunately I didn't notice Rudy's water glass until it was too late. Lucky for me he wasn't sitting there when I spilled it all over his chair. That would have *really* made him mad.

"Here, I'll get that, K.C. honey," Linda deftly swept the water into a handful of paper napkins and slid the soggy mess to one side while Julian sat down.

"Sorry about that." I blushed at my own clumsiness but Julian waved my apology aside. He had opted for a seafood dinner and I eyed his plate thoughtfully, wondering whether kinkajous ate shellfish.

"How's Topés?"

"She's fine. Ate half a banana and two slices of fish."

"She's lucky you rescued her, K.C." Julian complimented me and I shrugged modestly. "Or him," he finished pensively, remembering that we had not yet determined the kinkajou's gender.

"Hey Julian, thanks again for taking the time to show us Chichén Itzá," Linda said sincerely. "I got some great shots of you for the feature."

"It was my pleasure, believe me," Julian smiled warmly at all of us. "Where's Rudy?"

"Hormone attack," I replied briefly.

"He's calling his girlfriend in Montreal," Father elaborated.

"Pamela?" Julian had obviously been the recipient of a description of Rudy's love interest and we all sighed.

"Pamela," Linda nodded and there was silence for a while as we finished our meals. I studied Julian surreptitiously out of the corner of my eye. He was eating quite rapidly, wolfing his food down actually, and it looked like he was in a tearing hurry.

"Got any plans for the evening?" I asked him, supercasually, trying to find out whether he planned to work overtime with Beau and Billy Joe. Julian turned a rather surprised look on me. Actually, Father and Linda did too.

"Why? You have something in mind, K.C.?" Julian leered playfully at me and I blushed at the misunderstanding.

"Oh, uh, that's not what I meant, I just meant, um —" I cast a desperate look around and Linda came to my rescue.

"We were thinking of going to the town square tonight, you know, the *zócalo*. There's going to be a concert. You could come too, if you like, right K.C.?" Of course that wasn't what I'd meant at all but I nodded gratefully.

"Sure, that's it," I gulped. Julian shook his head.

"I'm afraid I have to hang around here. I have some paperwork to catch up on tonight, but maybe another time," he finished regretfully and I narrowed my eyes a little, wondering how I could gracefully segue from that topic to people working overtime on reconstructing Mayan ruins.

"K.C., you're bleeding," Julian was staring at me worriedly and following the direction of his gaze I noticed that the cherries had leaked through the napkin and right through the front of my shirt.

"It's just a little snack for later," I pulled out a cherry to demonstrate but Julian was still eyeing me with concern.

"What have you got there?" he pointed. I glanced down and realized that I should have used plastic bags instead of napkins, because the fish had leaked too. Father sighed and shook his head, smiling a little at me.

"Topés," he explained in a word. "K.C.'s been stashing food for her in her pockets." I flushed, embarrassed that they'd noticed.

"Well, she was hungry," I defended myself, "a growing kinkajou has to eat a lot, you know."

"Maybe we can work out a deal with the cook," Linda suggested, "he'd probably be willing to put some food aside for Topés if you asked him." I nodded, carefully re-wrapping the fish.

"I'll ask him tomorrow."

"Listen, I hate to eat and run like this but I have to go," Julian said and stood up. "See you later." After he left, we returned to the apartment where I unloaded the food I'd brought for Topés into her food dish. I was pleased to see her up and about, sniffing curiously at the confines of the box. On an impulse I reached in and picked her up, hoping that she wouldn't bite me now that she was rested.

Topés watched me with bright golden eyes and sniffed my fingers a little before apparently deciding that I was all right. I cuddled her quietly on the sofa, while watching a movie in Spanish with English subtitles. After a while Topés got curious and explored the sofa, poking her long nose into the cushions and generally sniffing everything she (or he) came across.

With a booming "Hi," Rudy came bounding into the room, his face lit with a big, goofy smile and dropped onto the sofa without making even one disparaging remark. What a difference a call makes!

"Hey! Watch out for Topés!" I snatched my new friend back in time to avoid her untimely demise at Rudy's hands. (Or butt, actually).

"Huh?" Rudy looked at Topés. "Oh, sorry. How is the little —" he hesitated for a fraction of a second, "—gal." It was nice to have the old, cheerful Rudy back for a change and I smiled at him.

"Topés is fine, thanks. She's been eating a lot and I think she feels better."

"Huh." Rudy grabbed the remote control and began channel surfing automatically while humming a disjointed little tune. He seemed so happy that I refrained from scolding him for interrupting my movie. It wasn't that interesting anyway.

"So did you talk to Pamela?" I asked politely, even though it was obvious that he had.

"She's great," Rudy replied, still smiling. "She misses me, too," he said with a touch of pride. "And guess what?" I sighed, already regretting that I'd brought the subject up.

"What?"

"We're going to the opera when I get back. Mozart's Magic Flute." I studied him closely, amazed. Yes, he was still my older brother, the one I'd heard refer to classical music as 'that boring old stuff.' The only explanation I could find for his sudden change of heart was that space aliens had taken control of his brain. Or The Lovely Pamela. Same thing, maybe.

"You know, that's what I like about her," Rudy continued, stretching himself comfortably on the sofa. I gently stroked Topés' soft fur and she nuzzled my hand. "She's an intellectual."

'Intellectual' was not quite the word I would have used to describe someone who spent over an hour a day on her hair (yes she did, she'd actually told me so) but Rudy seemed so happy that for once I couldn't bring myself to burst his bubble.

"I see." I stood up and carried Topés back to the box, where she was happy to settle in for another nap. Baby kinkajous sleep a lot, I guess.

Father and Linda came back from their walk on the beach just then, glowing and happy too.

"Anyone still want to go to the concert?" I asked.

"Me," Linda replied, wrapping both arms around Father's waist. She only comes up to his chin, and it looks really cute when they do that. "How about you, James?" Father smiled and hugged her back gently.

"Sure, why not. Did you talk to Pamela, Rudy?" he asked and Rudy nodded, still smiling.

"She's great," he repeated for the umpteenth time.

"It starts in a half hour, so we'd better go if we don't want to miss it." Linda tugged my Father toward the door and I followed along.

"I think I'll stay here and, um ..." Rudy glanced around the room as though seeing it for the first time, "... catch up on some reading or something." We left him there on the sofa, gazing dreamily at the evening news.

Isla Mujeres was charming in the evening, the sunset fading into murky purple and the heat of the day into pleasant warmth. People were out in droves, relaxing after work, eating ice cream and generally enjoying themselves. Father, Linda and I walked down Avenida Vincente Guerrero, turned right and walked three more blocks toward the square at the eastern end of town.

A little boy pedaled past us on a bike way too big for him. He had to stand to work the pedals and the seat reached clear up to his shoulders but he was having a wonderful time, or so it seemed from his smile.

Two elderly women sat on a stone bench under some pine trees, talking and fanning themselves lightly. They both wore sleeveless lace dresses embroidered with colors which seemed to glow in the semi-darkness over their dazzlingly white cotton shifts. They smiled at us and we smiled back at them. Everyone was in a fine mood and despite my apprehension I found myself relaxing, not completely, but enough to enjoy the gentle evening.

The town square was clearly the center of activity for the people of Isla Mujeres. The city hall stood diagonally across from the Immaculate Conception Church on the far corner. From the church itself came the sound of a full choir, singing glorious songs in Spanish. The church was already filled to capacity so we found a bench in the middle of the park where we could hear the music quite clearly.

In the very center of the park was a white stone pavilion where several children were chasing each other around in what appeared to be a game of dodge ball. Across the park was a trampoline where children shrieked joyfully, bouncing higher and higher into the air. I was thinking of taking a turn on the trampoline myself but then I spotted Billy Joe heading our way. So did Linda.

"Hi there, Billy Joe," she greeted him warmly and he looked startled at hearing his own name, glancing around nervously himself before he spotted us. "How's work coming on the project?" she continued. "Sorry we took Julian away for a whole day." Billy Joe shrugged, fiddling with the ever-present cigarette in his hand.

"That's all right, we made out without him just fine." His gaze slid over me briefly and I couldn't help noticing that his smile didn't quite reach his eyes.

"Hey, I was wondering if it would be all right for me to visit the site sometime and take some pictures of the statue you guys found the other day," Linda suggested brightly and Billy Joe turned a puzzled look on her.

"Statue?" he repeated, obviously confused by Linda's request. "What statue?"

"You know, the one of Ixchel." Linda is nothing if not patient in the line of duty.

"We didn't find no statue." Billy Joe shook his head but I reminded him.

"Julian told us that you found a statue of Ixchel at the site. You were about to tell us about it at dinner the other night, remember?" Billy Joe brushed a hand impatiently through his hair.

"No one found any statue, kid," he told me curtly. "All we found out there was a bunch of rocks. And then more rocks," he added, smiling a little at his own wit.

There was a pause as Linda and Father exchanged baffled looks, unable to reconcile Julian's description of the statue with Billy Joe's flat denial of its existence.

I, on the other hand, was smelling a rat. If Billy Joe said he didn't know anything about the statue that Julian told us they'd found then someone was lying and I was willing to bet that it was Billy Joe.

"Well, it was nice seeing you folks. I gotta go," Billy Joe said abruptly, and hurried off without even waiting for our reply.

Chapter Eight

"That's funny," Linda said slowly, "there must be some mistake."

"Yeah," I muttered, "when *he* was born." Father bent a reproving look on me.

"Be nice, K.C."

"Well it's true," I returned defensively, wishing that I could tell them about Billy Joe's connection to Señor Colón. I knew better than to say anything about that, though, for fear they'd have me on a shrink's couch the next day.

"Even if it were true, which it isn't, that doesn't mean you should go around saying things like that," Father pointed out reasonably. "There are all kinds of people in the world." I supposed that was so but it still didn't change my feelings.

"I wonder why Julian even works with someone like him?" I mused aloud. "I mean, Julian's so cool and Billy Joe's so... Neanderthal." Linda smiled.

"K.C., one thing you learn in life is there's no accounting for people. Billy Joe is probably a very talented archaeologist in his own right, otherwise he wouldn't even be assigned to the restoration project."

"Either that or they decided to take the brains/brawn approach in hiring. And Julian's the brains." In spite of himself, Father grinned a little at my wit.

I watched Billy Joe disappear into the distance. He was walking with such urgency that he bumped into the little boy on the bike, knocking the kid over without even a backward look or an apology. To me it seemed as though the big creep definitely had someplace else to be.

"Say, I'm feeling sort of tired," I announced suddenly, yawning widely to prove it. "I think I'll go back to the hotel now."

"Are you sure you'll be all right? You know how to get home from here?" Linda was as concerned for my well-being as if we'd been in the middle of New York City or something, where people think there are muggers around every corner.

"I'll be fine. You two have fun and don't stay out too late or you're both grounded for a week," I laughed over my shoulder, strolling in the same direction as that taken by Billy Joe.

"Very funny, K.C." Father called after me and I turned to sketch a brief bow in their direction. It isn't easy being the humorous one in the family, but someone has to do it.

Billy Joe was walking really fast, at odds with the relaxed pace of the people around him. I saw more than one person turn to stare after him curiously as I shadowed him down the street. After a few blocks it became apparent that he was heading for the hotel so I slowed my pace a little, trying to stay far enough behind him so as to not be too obvious about the way I was skulking along in his wake.

A man selling hand-tooled leather goods made a brief attempt to interest me in his wares but I just smiled and kept walking. Business before pleasure. Billy Joe reached the hotel just as I rounded the corner on Matamoros, and I was surprised to see that Beau was waiting for him in a pickup truck which was parked in front.

Very carefully I sauntered down the street toward them, pretending an interest in the closed shops around me and wishing I dared to get close enough to hear what they were saying. After a brief conversation, Billy Joe got into the truck and Beau started the engine, driving past the spot where I was hiding in a doorway and disappearing into the night. Curiouser and curiouser.

I stood there watching their taillights fade into the darkness, wondering whether it would be possible to catch a taxi and follow them. There were none around, and just then Rudy called out, "Hey K.C."

He was sitting at a white wrought iron table, feet propped up comfortably on the stone railing which ran around the big tiled veranda outisde the hotel lobby.

"How was the concert?" He seemed so amiable that I was glad to drop into the chair beside him. To tell the truth, my feet were a little tired from hiking around Mayan ruins all day.

"It was nice. The church was full but we found a bench outside and the music was really moving. Say, Rudy, did you see Billy Joe and Beau here a minute ago?" Rudy shrugged.

"They just left, why?"

"No reason. We saw Billy Joe in the park. Did you talk to them at all?" Rudy reached for the can of soda on the table and started to give me a funny look.

"I talked to Beau for a minute while he was waiting for Billy Joe. Why?"

"Did they say where they were going, by chance?" I pressed him for details and Rudy gave me a disapproving frown, changing abruptly back into his cranky alter-ego.

"You're doing it again, Kook Case."

"I am not! What?" I replied double-defensively.

"You're snooping around again, aren't you? You think you've found a mystery and now," he shook his head in frustration, "you just have to get to the bottom of it. I hate it when you do this to our vacations." It was an utterly unfair criticism, since my hunches were usually right. I mean, how could he blame *me* for the fact that other people do weird things?

"This is different," I explained patiently.

"You always say that," he reminded me peevishly, "when are you going to outgrow this phase of playing detective?" Despite my irritation at having my talents referred to as a 'phase', I persisted.

"Rudy, I'm serious, there's something going on here that's not right."

"All right then, tell me about it," Rudy invited, leaning back in his chair while I outlined my observations. When I had finished, he dismissed my suspicions.

"My bet is there's an easy explanation for the whole thing. Now let's examine the facts. You couldn't have seen Señor Colón the other day, since he's in jail, but you *thought* you saw him and that got you started imagining things. So you followed a couple of guys around, picking up bits and pieces of their conversation, and decided there's some mystery," Rudy continued irritably. "There's no mystery here, Kook Case. That 'Boss' guy Beau was talking to is probably just a rich banker who lent them money for the dig and Billy Joe and Beau are probably going to a party somewhere right now. Two grown men out for a night on the town. No mystery, end of story." Rudy sounded pretty sure of himself.

"What about the statue?" I persisted and Rudy sighed, pushing his hair back from his eyes wearily as he gave me a patronizing look meant to convey the infinite wisdom of his (almost) eighteen years.

"Oh come on, K.C. Billy Joe drinks, we know that. He might not even remember the statue, or maybe thought it was something else. I mean, get a grip, you're making too much of it."

"Huh." I folded my arms on my chest and thought about it. Despite being totally wrong in general, Rudy had brought up an interesting point. Actually, maybe Billy Joe had a drug problem. My experiences in Puerto Vallarta a few months earlier had given me firsthand knowledge of *that* sort of stuff.

"I wonder if the statue could be valuable?" I mused. "Remember? Julian told us about how careful they have to be with artifacts, and if Billy Joe has a drug problem he might have sold the statue or something and doesn't want Julian to know." Rudy stood up angrily, trying to win the argument by talking the loudest.

"Knock it off, K.C.! Why don't you give us all a break for a change and relax instead of scaring up trouble just because you're bored!" It was an entirely untrue accusation and I stood up and raised my voice a few decibels too, tired of justifying myself in the face of his obvious emotional reaction to my thoughtful analysis of the situation.

"Fine," I told him scornfully, "*be* that way."

"Me?!" Rudy said with an exasperated shake of his head, "*you're* the one with the problem! Anyway, if it bothers you so much, why don't you ask Julian, since you two are such," here he wiggled his eyebrows at me mockingly, "good friends." I stared at my brother in pure frustration and he stared back at me with a triumphant smile, as though he had proven his point. Turning away, I gave up the argument.

"Yeah, maybe I will go ask Julian. At least he listens to me." I stalked off, leaving Rudy there alone with his drink and his book.

There was a light on across the way, in the apartment where Julian, Billy Joe and Beau lived. I thought about it for a while then padded across the tiled hall to knock on the door. I didn't want to be a nuisance or anything but I sort of hoped that maybe Julian would be in. He was, and answered the door at my first knock, obviously expecting someone else.

Julian glanced up and down the hallway briefly then held the door open wider. "Oh, hi K.C., what's on your mind, would you like to come in?" I nodded (a bit nervously, I must admit) and followed him inside. I was intrigued to see that their apartment was the mirror image of ours, except that the color scheme of their place tended more toward the red/yellow end of the spectrum.

"It's a little cheery but you get used to it after a while," Julian grinned at me, obviously referring to the decor. "So what's up, K.C?" I paced nervously to the window, looking out over the town.

"Well, there's something funny going on," I told him bluntly.

"Funny how?" Julian asked blandly, adding, "would you like a drink or something?"

"No thanks, I'm fine. Well, we saw Billy Joe tonight and when Linda asked him about the statue you found he denied finding it," I frowned at Julian. "He said you guys hadn't found any statue at all, just a bunch of rocks." Julian was watching me with a look of true concern and when he finally spoke he said slowly,

"So he completely denied its existence?" I nodded.

"And that's not all, I sort of overheard them talking about putting in some overtime —" I began but Julian held up a hand, frowning.

"Whoa there, K.C. Start at the beginning please. You heard who talking?"

"I was on the patio and Beau and Billy Joe were talking near me. I heard Beau tell Billy Joe that they were going to have to work overtime. What if they're planning to sell the statue or something? I mean, you have to admit that it's odd the way Billy Joe pretended he didn't know anything about it." Julian's face paled slightly as I continued:

"And that's not all. Remember what I told you about catching that mobster, Señor Colón?" Julian nodded, slowly, watching me intently as I went on, "well the other day I saw Billy Joe talking to Señor Colón on his yacht, I think Billy Joe and Beau might be connected to whatever Señor Colón is up to, maybe he's the one they're going to sell the statue to or something and that's why they're working overtime."

"Now K.C.," Julian leveled a piercing stare at me, addressing me quite seriously, "if what you say is true then the situation may be quite dangerous. I don't want you to get involved in this, all right? Let me handle things from here. I want you to leave this completely alone while I find out what's going on. Stay away from Beau and Billy Joe from now on, all right?"

"I just thought you should know," I told him quietly as Julian ushered me firmly toward the door.

"I'm glad you shared your concerns with me and I promise I'll look into this right away, K.C." His touch was considerate, warm on my shoulder and I was distracted from my concerns by the sensation. Before I could figure out what was bothering me Julian released me gently.

"Remember, not another word to anyone else. Our best bet is to keep this thing quiet until I can find out what's going on."

"Mum's the word," I promised, slipping out the door. Julian gave me the thumbs-up sign and I returned to our apartment, feeling vastly relieved. It was good to know that Julian took my observations seriously enough to at least check into them, unlike a certain brother I could mention.

Chapter Nine

The next day dawned clear and bright with just a touch of haze. By the time I awoke and got dressed, Father and Linda were already up and talking about their plans for the day. I stumbled sleepily into the living room, squinting at the bright light of day.

"Good morning K.C.!" Rudy observed sarcastically, "you look all ready for a brand new day." Father and Linda looked at me, then at each other and I saw Linda hide a smile.

"Good morning," I replied politely, ignoring Rudy's attempt to harass me. Rudy knows that I'm already well aware that I'm not my best in the morning but he likes to remind me of it frequently. My brother, the sadist.

"We thought we'd try out that little place on the waterfront," Father said, "and get coffee and breakfast there for a change." I yawned agreement.

"Sounds good." After I had taken care of Topés we all went out into the street, then headed southwest on Matamoros until we reached the Avenida Gustavo Rueda Medina and the small waterfront café.

We got seats by the pier, and after scrutinizing our surroundings carefully to be sure that there was no white yacht nearby nor any diabolical strangers in the area, I began watching with interest as the passenger ferry discharged a load of tourists. There were about forty of them, and all were wearing one type or another of the casual, brightly-colored outfits which are the uniform of tourists everywhere.

A big white billboard on the pier advertised the ferry departure and arrival times. It looked like the boats ran every thirty minutes to Puerto Juárez, across the bay. As I sipped my fruit juice and looked out over the water, I began to actually wake up and enjoy the day.

Linda and Father were deciding between visiting Cancún for a day, or maybe visiting Playa Del Carmen which was a popular beach spot south of Cancún on Mexico 307. Linda was inclined toward Playa Del Carmen. Apparently there was another set of ruins at the site of Xcaret she wanted to check out. Not only that, she said, but she and Father could also take a ferry to a small island off the southern Yucatán coast called Cozumel where there were more ruins, and perhaps something she could use for her article.

I could see that Father wasn't too keen on the prospect of doing another full day trip south, especially after our exertions of the previous day. But I could also see the fond light in his eyes when he smiled at Linda. It was a milder variation of Rudy's goofy grin around Pamela.

"I suppose we could manage it, why not?" Father told her indulgently and Linda grinned in response.

"Thanks, darling. You won't regret it. How about you two?" she smiled at me and Rudy. Rudy cocked his head sideways then shook it, glancing from Linda to Father regretfully.

"I don't think so, if it's all right with you two I really do want to go snorkeling."

"How about you, K.C.?" Father asked me in turn. I shook my head at them both.

"Sorry, I thought I'd hang out here too, maybe go check out some of the sights or something."

"Well." Linda seemed slightly disappointed but she smiled anyway. "I'm sure you two will have a good time. We'll take lots of pictures to show you when we get back." I'll go reserve the car, James." She then went in search of a phone.

I concentrated on the omelette I'd had the chef make me. The fluffy eggs smothered in salsa mexicana were delicious. By the time Linda returned I had nearly finished breakfast and felt much better.

"Well, I guess we'd better get going," Linda said to Father. "We'll take the ferry to Puerto Juárez and pick up our rental car in downtown Cancún." Father stood up with a tiny sigh.

"See you kids later, then. Dinner at eight?" Father cocked an eyebrow at me and Rudy and we nodded in agreement. "Good. Now take care, you two, and remember, no fighting."

We paid the very reasonable *cuenta*, and then Father and Linda hurried to board the ferry just before it pulled away from the pier, leaving behind a frothy green wake in the clear crystal water of the bay.

Rudy and I strolled back to the hotel, debating the course of our day. Although neither one of us really wanted to be around the other we decided to split the cost of renting a golf cart for a day, then drive it to Garrafón National Park, which is famous for its snorkeling. I would drop Rudy off there and take the cart across the island for a look at the Hacienda Mundaca, listed in my guide book as the mansion built by Señor Mundaca for the lady who scorned his love.

Rudy squinted at me doubtfully when I told him of my plans but said nothing, and we puttered about the apartment for a while, getting ready. I hurried downstairs and asked Agustín, the cook, for the big cardboard box his paper towels had come in. He gave me a strange look, but honored my request.

When I mentioned that I had a need for small quantities of foods being set aside he squinted at me shrewdly, and when I allowed as how I might have a kinkajou to feed, his face split into a broad grin and he gave the box a comprehending nod.

"*¡Bueno!* Señorita has the pet kinkajou. I give the food, you come back later, OK?" I smiled and thanked him, then left, box in hand.

Topés was happy to be transferred into a larger container. I had thought earlier about letting her run around my room in my absence but decided I didn't know enough about kinkajous to imagine what kind of trouble she might get into.

I put her into the new, larger box and she trotted happily around in it, sniffing here and there before returning to her food and water dishes. I think she smiled at me as she ate the leftover omelette I'd saved her.

"Ready, K.C.?" I nodded and followed Rudy from the hotel. We headed south on Matamoros to Avenida Hidalgo, took a left, then walked a few blocks to the Restaurant Bar el Sombrero de Gomar.

It was an easy place to spot since there was a long row of golf carts lined up along the street near the corner where the restaurant was located. A small fleet of mopeds were available for hire as well, parked next to the golf carts which were dark green with white numbers painted across the sides.

For ninety pesos an hour Rudy and I arranged to have cart number four at our disposal all day. We headed out along busy Avenida Gustavo Rueda Medina which took us southeast along the island toward Garrafón beach. Driving the cart was really challenging right along the waterfront, as there was a lot of traffic on the road. More than once I was actually glad that Rudy was at the wheel.

Once we got past the Port Authority at the far end of town things calmed right down and we had the road nearly to ourselves, save for the occasional taxi or fellow golf cart enthusiast. We passed the airstrip and headed through lush fields, thick with bushes and perfumed with the heavy odor of ripe tropical vegetation. It was the same road Julian, Linda and I had taken going home the day before and I recognized a few landmarks along the way.

It smelled like the air itself was wearing perfume, and as Rudy slowed to turn a corner I heard insects buzzing loudly, their calls resonating in the heat of the day. Rudy sped up again and we passed a small town on our left, a jumble of colorful stucco houses built up into the hills which sloped away on the other side toward the sea.

I saw one or two of the locals glance at us with amusement as we whizzed by on our cart and thought to myself that it must have been quite a transition for the peaceful people of Isla Mujeres when the tourist industry came to the island.

On my left I caught a glimpse of a road leading to a broad white beach, the kind of beach used in suntan lotion ads, but it wasn't Garrafón Beach. A sign proclaimed it to be Playa Lancheros. According to the map I consulted, Garrafón Beach was just a little way down the road from the ruins of Ixchel. I thought about that for a moment as Rudy pulled into a parking lot overlooking a broad expanse of bay.

"Here we are," Rudy spoke for the first time as he handed me the key to the golf cart, adding, "Don't lose it, OK?" He sounded as annoyed as though I had already lost it and I scowled at him, clipping it onto my key chain.

"How 'bout I just swallow it for safe-keeping then, bro', would that do?"

"Sure, right. Don't do anything stupid, either. Stay on the back roads and drive carefully." I could see that Rudy had *mucho* reservations about leaving the golf cart in my more than capable hands, even though his mind was already somewhere else.

"Don't worry, Rudy, I'll be fine." Such a worrier, my dear brother!

We eyed each other warily for a moment, then, after agreeing to meet me in two hours, Rudy paid the admission lady 15 pesos to enter Garrafón National Park.

"Don't be late," he admonished me as he turned away.

I watched from the parking lot as he made his way toward the locker rooms. There were signs posted along the walkway he followed, advising snorkelers to shower before entering the water, as sunblock products could kill the coral reef.

Further down near the water a series of rocks, like steps, led into the snorkeling area where people in swim suits and swim shoes floated face down in the gentle waves, marveling at the beauty of the reef. I knew from experience that the swim shoes were necessary, since in some places the coral was razor-sharp.

Some of the snorkelers were feeding the fish what looked like bread crumbs, and I watched with interest as a big silver fish leaped from the water to snatch something from the hand of a middle-aged man in green and yellow bathing trunks. Laughing, he turned and smiled to see that his wife had captured the moment on film.

Down along the water's edge I spotted a mask and fin rental shop, a cafe and many *palapas*, the thatched little grass-roofed beach umbrellas under which an assortment of people lounged, laughing and talking. It looked like fun and I planned to join Rudy as soon as I took care of my other plans for the day.

I wasn't intending to spy on anyone, you understand, but if I just happened to be driving the golf cart past the temple (which, after all, was right around the corner), it would be ridiculous not to even stop and say hello to Julian and the gang.

In fact it would be downright un-neighborly. Feeling altruistic, I bought a few big bottles of cold orange juice at a nearby concession stand and put them in the little cooler Rudy and I had brought along with us, thinking that perhaps my archaeologist friends would like some refreshment.

Garrafón Beach was easily within walking distance of the lighthouse and Ixchel's temple but I took the golf cart anyway, enjoying the sensation of controlling the vehicle without having Rudy breathing down my neck. There was an abundance of other tourists on the road and I found myself becoming one of a long line of golf carts all heading in the same direction.

The small parking lot near the light house was already crowded to capacity with a mixture of moped, golf carts and bicycles, so I parked further back from the crowd and walked down the short dirt road leading to the lighthouse where a small crowd of tourists had stopped to take pictures.

Julian and Beau were working hard on the temple in the hot sun and welcomed me with sighs then smiles when I handed them the juice bottles. There was no sign of Billy Joe so I left an extra one for him in the shade.

"K.C., you're a real life saver," Julian said, and popped his bottle open right away, taking a healthy swallow. "This is perfect, thanks."

"It's a pleasure," I replied, studying them both surreptitiously. Julian was sporting a day's growth of beard and it looked as though he hadn't shaven since the last time I'd spoken with him. Beau, too, had a rumpled look and he was wearing dark glasses so I couldn't see his eyes but Julian's were red-rimmed and shadowed.

I strolled toward the ruins to stand where I had been two days before. To me, Ixchel's temple seemed to be in the same state of disrepair it had been in when I'd seen it last. I frowned at the numbered block by my foot. It bore the exact same numerical sequence I'd seen last time.

"So," I spoke over my shoulder to Julian and Beau who were still leaning against a wall in the shade of the ruins, sipping juice, "been working hard on the reconstruction?" Beau nodded and grim lines appeared around his mouth. It didn't look like he was suppressing a smile.

"We've been making some real progress, too," he told me quite seriously. I licked my lips, looking down at the untouched rows of stone blocks.

"Pretty soon the temple will be in its original state, huh?" I asked innocently and Julian caught my eye.

"Pretty soon. Say, come here, K.C. I have something I want to show you." Julian left the sanctuary of the shade and draped a friendly arm across my shoulders, steering me toward the rocky promontory where we'd stood before. Instinctively, I looked out to sea, hoping to spot the orange buoy I'd seen before, but there was no sign of it now.

"What are you doing here?" Julian asked me tersely as soon as we were away from Beau. I gave him a startled glance, then shrugged.

"I dropped Rudy off at Garrafón beach. Since I was in the neighborhood, I thought I'd stop by. I'm on my way to Hacienda Mundaca from here." That, at least, was entirely the truth, and I met Julian's eyes squarely. "Why?"

"Well," Julian looked away from me briefly, "I was afraid you might be —" He paused delicately, perhaps sensitive to wounding my feelings.

"Snooping around?" I supplied, then grinned at him unabashedly. "Well, now that you mention it, did you get a chance to check on that statue?" Julian sighed and as he ran a hand tiredly through his hair and his face took on that look that adults get when they are tired of kid stuff.

"K.C., I thought we had agreed to let me handle things here."

"I was just wondering, Julian." (It was my turn to feel embarrassed.) "Look, I'm sorry for interrupting you. I didn't mean to be a nuisance." Julian shook his head at me, a half smile on his lips.

"It's not that you're a nuisance, K.C., but we really do have a lot to accomplish here and I'd appreciate it if you'd let me take care of things at this end. I promise you I'll keep you updated, all right?"

I was standing facing the sea and Julian was leaning against the rocks in front of me when my eyes caught a movement in the water about two hundred yards out from the cliffs below. I blinked and squinted at the water again, but now there was nothing.

"K.C., are you all right?" Something of my surprise must have shown on my face, for Julian was watching me a little uneasily. For a split second I debated telling him what I'd just seen, but then dismissed the idea. After all, he'd just given me a lecture on staying out of things.

"I'm sorry, my mind was wandering a little there," I replied easily. "Say, I really should be going, I'll just let you get back to work." Julian escorted me back to the lighthouse. He tried not to show it but I could tell he was relieved to see me go.

"See you later then," he waved me out of sight and I drove slowly around a curve in the road then turned off the road and stopped the golf cart, thinking about my options. I wanted to get a closer look at the shoreline near the cliffs, because something odd was certainly happening down there. The Hacienda Mundaca would just have to wait for another day.

Chapter Ten

I found a pseudo-parking spot for the golf cart under a big clump of red-flowered bushes in a small recess by the road and headed cross-country style toward the water line.

The grass grew thickly underfoot, like a tufted mat, and I had to pick my way through carefully so as not to trip and fall. Cacti fought with scrawny bushes for tenancy among the rocks, and here and there were iguanas lying around taking the sun.

For the most part the big grey and black lizards regarded me with unmoving indolence, but those I disturbed slid off the rocks and disappeared into the thick brush at my approach. I reached the water's edge, and found myself about three hundred yards up from the bottom of the cliffs, which rose from the water like jagged white teeth, stained by countless tides.

I looked out to sea to where I'd seen the movement, but as luck would have it there was nothing there. Furthermore, it was hard for me to see with the glare of the sun on the water at that angle. Ideally, a person would want to study the place at sunset or dawn, and with a good pair of binoculars. I kicked myself for forgetting them.

I started walking along the rocky shore, picking my way through patches of crumbling limestone and sandstone. Shells crunched underfoot and I decided that the tide probably rose sufficiently to deposit them there. Either that or they must have some really awesome storms on the island.

I followed a slight bend in the coastline and was interested to see what lay behind the green plastic screen employed by the construction workers. They had built a big, ugly concrete block building about twenty yards from the cliff's edge.

I frowned, surprised to see that it had no windows and apparently only one, garage-like door. Whatever it was, it looked unappealingly utilitarian and distinctly at odds with the beauty of the coast.

I made my way slowly downward toward the water, my view of the construction work above mostly blocked by bushes growing along an overhang of low sandstone cliffs to my right. The cliffs were just beginning their rise to the sky and a little farther ahead of me they began their steep ascent to the pinnacle upon which rested Ixchel's temple.

I could have walked along the top of the ridge instead, but I wanted a clear view of the sea so I took the lower path, nearer to the water. It was tricky going, and on a few occasions I had to climb up and over several house-sized boulders which had apparently fallen from the side of the cliffs.

Below and to my left, the waves were no longer playful, but broke viciously on jagged chunks of black rock which poked through the water like deadly offshore islands. It was definitely not the kind of place for swimming, or diving, or even boating. I shuddered, imagining a sailboat getting caught in the waves and being dashed to pieces on the rocks.

I reached a huge outcropping of stone beyond which it was apparent that I could climb no further. I craned my neck and peered upwards. A glance at the cliff above telling me that I was directly below the construction site.

I sat down on top of a big rock and leaned my chin in my hand, thinking and watching the waves for anything unusual. It was cool and shady where I sat, a refreshing mist rose from the waves below and I relaxed a little, still keeping an eye out for anything and everything.

Finally, after about ten minutes of nothing, I got up to leave, when again I spotted a dark shape in the water, this time about a hundred yards from the cliffs.

I froze, watching as a big, black shape rose from the water. Seeming to hang in the air for a moment, it floated upward toward the cliff then disappeared as if it had melted right into the cliff wall. Oddly enough though, the point where it disappeared corresponded roughly to the spot directly above where I'd seen the orange buoy on my first visit to Ixchel's temple.

The sound of a car's engine reached my ears and for a moment I looked at the water in confusion, wondering where the sound was coming from. Then I realized the sound was above and behind me, coming from the construction site.

I scrambled carefully up the rocks, toward the top of the sloping cliff over my head. A big boulder at the cliff's edge provided cover for me and I crawled behind it, peering around cautiously toward the source of the noise. A car door slammed and to my surprise I saw Beau climbing out of a pickup truck he'd parked nearby. Even more surprising was the fact the Billy Joe was coming out of the newly constructed building to greet him.

"Hey." Beau lifted a hand in greeting.

"Hey." Billy Joe replied and I froze, wondering what the two of them could be doing up there. I crouched behind the boulder, watching curiously as Beau and Billy Joe stood smoking cigarettes by the door of the building.

Both men stood silently for a while, looking out at the horizon. Billy Joe rubbed his neck briefly as though it hurt, and turned to Beau with a frown.

"So, you hear anything?"

"Two days," Beau answered tersely. "Job's gotta be done in two days. Boss don't want to wait any longer, he's getting nervous." Beau looked sideways at Billy Joe. "Boss said Jorge saw that nosy kid with Julian the other day at a restaurant near Chichén Itzá. Wanted to know how Julian knew her." Billy Joe exhaled with a snort and ground his cigarette out mercilessly on the gravel beneath his foot.

"Must be that Flanagan kid, what's her name, Jaycee?"

"K.C." Beau corrected him grimly, "yeah, that's what I figured too. Guess I'll tell Jorge, have him check it out." I felt cold with terror. Once Señor Colón found out where I was staying I would never be safe.

"So how's it going down there?" Beau changed the subject abruptly. Billy Joe shook his head in disgust, wiping sweat from his forehead with his sleeve.

"Generator broke down again."

"Again?" Beau scowled, "gonna take long to fix it?"

"Nope," Billy Joe shook his head, "got it up and running again." I watched them both cautiously as they finished their cigarettes in silence. Finally Billy Joe turned away with a weary groan and opened the door to the building behind him.

"Later."

"Yeah." Beau returned to the Chevy and Billy Joe disappeared inside the building.

I sat down again, puzzling over what I'd seen. I thought about things for a while and when I remembered to check the time and saw I was already ten minutes late to pick up Rudy.

A man's voice startled me. *"¡Señorita! ¡Hola, señorita!"* I glanced up to see a young man staring at me, a serious expression on his face. I stood up hastily, brushing myself off and wondering how I could explain the fact that I was hiding behind a big rock on what was no doubt private property.

"My foot," I explained quickly, gesturing at one sandal, "I stubbed my toe on a rock." It was a pretty weak excuse so I limped a little as though actually injured, pantomiming great pain.

"Stobbed, what means stobbed?" he repeated in some confusion, obviously not familiar with the term.

"Bumped," I added, and kicked the ground with my other foot, intending to clarify things, but his frown only deepened and he shook his head again.

"Bomp?" From the way he was dressed I would have guessed him to be one of the construction workers I'd seen the other day. In fact he looked like the one who had waved to me earlier.

"No turismo en esto sitio," he told me, giving up his efforts to understand what I was saying. He looked from me to the pathway I'd followed then glanced nervously over his shoulder, *"está* private property. *Propiedad privada.* Go, *señorita!"* He made a shooing gesture toward me, obviously inviting me to vacate the premises. I tried out my best smile on him.

"Sorry, I didn't know I was trespassing. Say, what is that thing you're building there?" I gestured to the big concrete structure nervously, hoping that Billy Joe wouldn't choose this moment to come outside for another smoke break. The young man's face relaxed slightly and he shrugged, then smiled back.

"*No hablo inglés.* Go 'way, *señorita, por favor.*" He calmed down somewhat but the message was still clear: I was to leave. I turned to go, sensing that if I didn't go voluntarily he would probably take my arm and escort me personally.

"*Lo siento, disculpa me*" I told him as I preceded him up to the dirt road where I'd left the golf cart parked, "I'm sorry, please excuse me." He shrugged, actually smiling when he realized that I was going to leave without protest.

"*Adiós, señorita.*" He was cute when he smiled, too bad it was because he was so clearly glad to see me go. I felt mildly deflated that I was having this effect on people lately. I mean, first Julian and then this guy, so happy to shoo me away.

I drove away and headed straight back to Garrafón beach for my rendezvous with Rudy. Along the way I puzzled over my recent discoveries. I still hadn't figured things out by the time I reached Garrafón beach.

I checked my watch again. I was only fifteen minutes late, an excusable margin of error, but when I pulled into the parking lot Rudy was already there, waiting for me with barely-concealed irritation.

"Where have you been?" Before I could even say a word he was on my case. "I thought I told you not to be late!" Rudy glared at me. He was wiggling his shoulders in a strange way under the lightweight cotton shirt he wore.

"I'm sorry, Rudy, I really am," I apologized, "but it's only fifteen minutes, right?"

"It's the principle of the thing," he insisted testily, shrugging strangely again.

"What's wrong?" I asked, concerned by his weird new mannerism.

"Nothing," he replied, but for the first time I noticed that the skin of his neck was burned a dark, angry red.

"Rudy, you're sunburned, let me see."

"It's nothing," he repeated firmly, "now give me the keys already." I handed him the keys to the cart, saying nothing. The only thing worse than lovesick Rudy is Rudy when he's just plain sick. And if the rest of his skin was as red as the part I could see he for sure wasn't feeling well.

"I guess I might have stayed in the water longer than I should have," Rudy mumbled, starting the golf cart gingerly. "I saw a Spanish shipwreck under water," he added. "It was cool. How was the Hacienda Mundaca?"

"Actually I never made it there," I told him casually.

"Where exactly did you go instead?" he wanted to know. I hesitated, choosing my words carefully.

"I went for a walk."

"Come on K.C. don't play games, where did you go?" The last thing I wanted was to fight with my lovesick, sunburned and naturally overbearing brother. I evaded the question.

"I just went for a walk along the cliffs. Can't I just go for a walk sometimes if I want to?"

"If it were anyone else asking me that I'd have to say yes but knowing you K.C., the answer is no." Rudy smirked, then resumed his line of questioning: "So what were you looking for down there?"

"Where?" I really didn't want to tell Rudy what I'd seen, he would simply dismiss my observations as the product of an overactive imagination and then we'd just end up fighting again.

"Cut it out K.C., you're not getting out of it like that," Rudy snapped. "I know you're up to something, you have that 'look' you get." I decided to take a chance on explaining.

"Oh all right, I'll tell you, but I bet you won't believe me. I went down by the cliffs because the other day I saw an orange buoy, remember I told you?"

"Did you see anything else?"

"As a matter of fact I also saw something come up out of the water and melt into the cliff."

" 'Melted' into the cliff, did it? Like grilled cheese?" Rudy snickered impolitely, despite himself. "Maybe it was a hologram mermaid. Or wait, don't tell me, Neptune himself on a decal?"

"Actually, you ignoramus, that would be the Mayan god Ah Cantzicnal," I corrected him coldly. "Or wait, would it be Ah Itzam?" I debated the point with myself; the latter god was a water witch whereas the former was an aquatic deity. "Maybe Ahpua, God of fishing," I mused, but Rudy didn't care about the jurisdictions of ancient Mayan gods and turned a very serious, older-brother type look on me.

"Look K.C., the thing is, just because you've solved a few mysteries in the past, now you think everyone around you is up to something," he explained firmly. "You're starting to project." I studied him thoughtfully, wondering if he would believe me if I told him about overhearing Billy Joe and Beau.

"The thing is," I decided to go for it, "I saw Señor Colón the other day and his pal Jorge chased me, remember?"

"Uh, huh. R-i-g-h-t." Rudy gave me a look of flat disbelief so I added quickly,

"And then today I overheard Billy Joe and Beau talking about how Jorge saw us at Chichén Itzá, remember? Jorge was the guy in the white car." Rudy gave me a doubtful glance.

"There was no white car, or have you forgotten, secret agent double-oh-Flanagan?" Ha-ha. Rudy was now rolling his eyes like Rodney Dangerfield and humming the theme song of the last James Bond movie.

"Well, maybe *you* didn't see it but I did!" I insisted and he sighed, wincing a little as he shifted gingerly in his seat.

"Look, K.C., trust me. You're going off the deep end on this." I gazed at him in reproach.

"How can you not believe me?"

"Because, you're losing it," my older brother told me flatly. I shook my head firmly at him.

"Am not."

"Are too. K.C., think about it, none of this can be happening, 'cause this Señor Colón guy is in jail. There goes your whole premise right there." His tone implied absolute certainty and as for me, I started to feel annoyed.

"You are so thick, Rudolph" I replied, tired of his insistent doubt. "You didn't believe me in Puerto Vallarta but I was right then, wasn't I?"

"That's not the point, that was then and this is now. You were so traumatized by what happened to you back then that now you're starting to project. You're imagining danger in every little thing, like the way you thought you saw Señor Colón that time we went white-water rafting."

"But I did see him, remember? I was right then and I'm just as right, now." I felt oddly betrayed by Rudy's attitude, even though I'd had an inkling of how he would react even before I told him. "You're just being mean because you're sunburned and because you miss Pamela," I said curtly.

Rudy bent an interested look on me. "Pamela? What does she have to do with your imagining things?" I knew full well that he knew what I meant but I repeated myself anyway.

"You just don't want to listen to anything I say because you're mad, because I—oh, never mind. Let's just drop it," I shrugged, seeming to concede the point.

"Don't take it that way, K.C." Rudy replied mildly. "I'm just trying to help you out. Father and Linda are really worried about you, you know."

"I know." I sighed. Rudy added soothingly,

"You know I'm always here for you if you need someone to talk to."

"No you're not," I muttered, "you won't even listen to me." Rudy lapsed into silence, probably thinking about Pamela since I had mentioned her which was fine with me. I had no intention of ever unburdening myself to my older brother again. Even though he meant well, he didn't take me seriously enough to even consider that what I was saying might be true.

Downtown Isla Mujeres was busy with the usual tourist traffic but I was able to get us safely to the Restaurant Bar Gomar where Rudy and I dropped off the golf cart, with fifteen minutes to spare.

"Muchas gracias," the rental agent told us as we handed him the key. *"¿Está bien?"* I nodded back at him cheerfully.

"Muy bien, gracias a usted." Rudy and I turned to leave and were crossing the street when I snapped my fingers, exclaiming,

"Hang on a second Rudy, wait here, I think I left my map in the golf cart." I hurried back to the restaurant to see the rental agent. His smile was tinged with curiosity as I spoke:

"Señor, por favor, I would like to rent the cart again tomorrow." He squinted at me assessingly and nodded.

"Mañana. Sí, señorita."

"I'll be by to pick it up at," I braced myself to utter the words, "six a.m., if that's all right with you." I thought the man gulped a little but then he nodded, possibly since I handed him a wad of cash for half of the down payment. He smiled, frowned a bit, then nodded as he wrote out my receipt.

Getting an early start on the day, especially *that* early, would be a definite challenge, but I had to have a look at the construction site when no one else was around. Knowing the relaxed pace of life here on the island, I was willing to bet that the site would be deserted at that hour.

"Mi esposa will meet you here," the man told me, serenely committing his wife to the task. *"Mañana por la mañana,* six a.m." We nodded to each other like conspirators, which in a way we were, and he handed me the receipt. I wondered what his wife would have to say when he told her she would be rising before dawn the next day to rent a golf cart to a crazy *turista*.

Chapter Eleven

When I caught up with him, Rudy didn't even ask me if I'd found the fictional map I'd claimed to have left behind. He was hugging a patch of shade and scowling to himself and I could tell he was quite uncomfortable. I sighed because even though he could be a real jerk sometimes, Rudy was still my brother and I didn't enjoy seeing him in pain. There are things which transcend even a vicious sibling quarrel, so I called a truce.

"You all right?" I asked. He eyed me resentfully, shrugged, then winced.

"I think so, yeah," but he didn't look all right to me. He'd wrapped a light towel casually across the back of his neck to keep the sun from burning him further, but I could see the fibers of the towel were really irritating his skin.

"Rudy," I headed towards a small store selling straw hats in different shapes and sizes, "come here a minute." I selected a white panama hat with a moderately wide brim. It was adorned with a dashing black satin ribbon and was clearly designed for a man. I paid the vendor fifty pesos for it as Rudy watched, puzzled.

"K.C., you already have a hat," he reminded me, very slowly and carefully, perhaps thinking that I'd forgotten it was right up there on my head.

"I know," I returned, equally patiently, "but this isn't for me, it's for you." I plopped the hat onto his head before he could protest. "There. Looks quite sublime, don't you think?" Rudy scowled and lifted the hat right back off, obviously intending to return it to the rack. "Can't do that," I shook my head at him cheerfully. "It's too late, I already bought it. Just wear it already, it'll keep the sun off your neck, for crying out loud."

I started walking away without waiting for his response, and after a moment he caught up with me.

"Um, thanks, I guess," he mumbled to me, settling the hat cautiously atop his head. After a few steps he removed the towel with a sigh of relief.

When we arrived at the hotel we found a message from Father and Linda waiting for us at the front desk. They were returning later, at eight p.m. We were on our own until then, and they'd see us when they got back.

"I think I'll try a cold shower," Rudy told me, shifting his shoulders uncomfortably.

"Try taking some aspirin too," I nodded, "it'll ease the pain and —"

"I know, I know, it helps stop inflammation. You don't have to tell me what to do, I'm not —" Rudy had interrupted me impatiently but then stopped himself in mid-sentence, sheepishly glancing upwards at the brim of the hat. "All right, I admit, the hat was a good idea," he added gruffly and we smiled at each other for a brief moment. Then he went upstairs. It's weird how Rudy can be so creepy one minute then so great the next.

I went downstairs to pay a visit to Agustín, the hotel cook. He greeted me with a broad smile, beckoning me into the huge tiled kitchen to show me a big plate of food he'd saved for my little Topés.

"Wow, thanks!" I smiled at the assortment of fresh fruit, fish and milk he'd assembled. "How much do I owe you?" I would have paid him but he held up a hand in quasi-indignant protest.

"Es gratis," he informed me warmly but firmly. No amount of protest to the contrary would change his mind so in the end I gratefully accepted the food and took it upstairs for Topés.

She was waiting for me, her long orange and white striped tail curved delicately over her feet. She sat upright, watching me curiously as I wrapped half of the food in plastic for later and put the rest in the box for her.

To my surprise, she wasn't interested in the food, but strolled over to sniff intently at my hand. I thought I felt her lick one of my fingers and was so startled that I pulled my hand away quickly with a yelp. Topés regarded me with huge, reproachful golden eyes and sat down again, yawning widely.

"Oops, sorry pal, didn't mean to be rude there." Cautiously I extended my hand again and she resumed her exploration of my fingers.

"She seems pretty tame," Rudy commented as he emerged from the shower and spotted me crouched over Topés' box. "She's really quiet too, isn't she?" I nodded at him. It was true that I'd never heard Topés make a single sound.

"Did the shower help?" I asked Rudy, studying him closely. He was wearing nothing but a towel and, to my mild surprise, the panama hat. As I watched he turned to the glass mirror by the door and adjusted the hat slightly before giving himself an approving nod.

"I think so." The skin on his upper body had faded from an angry purplish color to dark red but it still looked like a serious burn. I glanced back down at Topés, who'd finally investigated the plate of food, then got to my feet.

"Join me for dinner downstairs?" I suggested, changing the topic.

"Let me get dressed first," he replied, as though I would have even considered letting him leave the apartment attired as he was.

"All right." Rudy disappeared into the bathroom.

I paused to reflect for a moment upon the fact that Rudy and I were, for once, not fighting. It was nice for a change, but I knew that it was only a matter of time before he said something sappy about The Lovely Pamela, and I wouldn't be able to resist joking about her. Or perhaps he would make some snide comment about my 'imagining things' and then we'd be back to square one, fighting again. Oh, well. *C'est la vie.*

I lounged on the sofa while I waited for Rudy, flipping idly through my guidebook about Isla Mujeres. For a small island it was pretty packed with neat things to do and I was reading up on legalized local gambling when Rudy rejoined me, dressed in jeans and a long-sleeved white cotton shirt.

"Ready to eat?" I asked, tossing the magazine back on the coffee table as I got to my feet. Rudy paused in front of the mirror by the door to tilt his hat to a rakish angle before following me. When we reached the lobby the desk clerk beckoned to us with an air of urgency.

"*Señor Rudy Flanagan?* Telephone call for you, *señor.* Long distance, from Canada."

"For me?" Rudy exclaimed, his whole face lighting up. "Just a minute, I'll take it. K.C. would you mind —"

"I know, I know. I'll save you a seat." I fluttered my hands at him, "Run along, and say 'hi' to her for me, all right?" He was gone at a run before I'd even finished speaking.

I took a table at the restaurant and sat down to order. By the time Rudy finished talking and came to join me, I had already finished my main course of smoked fish and was busy with the ice cream dessert.

Father and Linda returned from their adventures shortly after that, and went upstairs briefly to drop off their camera cases before joining Rudy and me in the restaurant.

"Oh, my aching feet," Linda murmured as she sank gratefully into a chair across from me, "I swear that guide had legs of steel. We walked for miles and he kept saying, 'it's just over this hill', 'it's just over this hill.' " She trailed off with a huge sigh and I raised an eyebrow at Father.

"I thought you rented a car?"

"We did," he nodded, "but the ruins on Cozumel were inaccessible. There was a tree down from a storm last week and it was blocking the road so we had to walk the last part of the way. We hired a local guide to take us there and I think he thought we were sissies," Father smiled a little.

"Sissies? Why?"

"It was quite a hike and we kept asking him —"

"How much farther is it?" Linda put in tiredly, "and he kept saying —"

"It's just over this hill." Father grinned, finishing her sentence for her. They smiled at each other and Linda chuckled.

"We must have walked for about ten miles that way, over dozens of hills... It was worth it though. The Temple of Ixchel on Cozumel is much larger than the one here on Isla Mujeres."

"It wasn't so bad," Father agreed, stretching his legs out cautiously, "but I think tomorrow would be a good day to take it easy."

"Definitely," Linda nodded fervently. "What did you two do, other than get extremely sunburned?" She finished on a more serious note, her gaze focusing intently on Rudy. "Look at Rudy, James."

"I see that," Father replied, getting that worried, parental look. "That looks like a pretty bad burn, Rudy. What happened?" Rudy shrugged, then grimaced unbecomingly.

"It was accidental. I went snorkeling and stayed out a little longer than I intended." He looked from Father to Linda, adding defensively, "It wasn't my fault really. They make you wash off your sunblock before you go into the water, because the chemicals in the sunblock can kill the reef."

"I see," Father said and exchanged a quick glance with Linda.

"I saw stuff from the wreck of a sunken Spanish trading ship. It's been there so long, parts of the reef are growing around it," Rudy explained quickly. "They were a little farther out from shore and I guess I just forgot how long I was out there."

"Well, it'll probably be all right." Linda was still studying Rudy with the practiced eye of a gifted amateur medic. She has been on enough photojournalistic expeditions to have first-hand experience with the hazards of travel.

In fact, it was after she broke her ankle on an expedition to the Himalayas that she took a course in first aid, and while I wouldn't call her a fanatical paramedic, I would say she has a compelling interest in the subject.

"I think I might have something to relieve the pain, Rudy. I'll check in a bit," Linda suggested, and he looked at her gratefully. Linda travels with a small supply of pharmaceuticals up to and including medicated eye drops for an injured cornea. She is very thorough.

"And how is little Topés?" Father's eyes crinkled into a warm smile for me. "Is she eating well?"

"I worked out a deal with the cook downstairs and he gave me a big plate of food for her. He wouldn't let me pay him but I guess I could give him a nice tip or something when we leave."

"That would be a good idea," Father replied. "The people here are very friendly, aren't they?" It was a rhetorical question but we all nodded anyway. The people on Isla Mujeres were, with few exceptions, the most easy-going folks I'd met abroad.

"Pamela called," Rudy remarked, "all the way from home." He said this so proudly that I couldn't stop myself from cracking wise.

"Imagine!" I said, as supercilious as I could manage, "She actually dialed the number all by herself!" Rudy's eyes narrowed ever so slightly.

"Well, her service put the call through, but it was her idea." The Lovely Pamela has an answering service which helps her arrange her many social appearances, both personal and telephonic.

"How nice," both Father and Linda nodded politely and when Rudy still seemed to be waiting for something, Father added, "Um, how is she?"

"Well," Rudy began, his face taking on a satisfied glow and I knew we were really in for it. Get him started when he's in that mode and you'll be there until he's talked you blue in the face.

"No wait, let's guess!" I suggested impulsively. "Don't tell us Rudy, she went shopping again today?" Rudy's eyes widened in surprise at the accuracy of my guess.

"How did you—?" he began but I held a hand up.

"And she bought the *cutest* outfit too!" I went on breezily. "It was even on sale so she got matching shoes and wait, let me guess, the *sweetest* little handbag, right?" I knew I was right when Rudy's look of confusion was slowly replaced by one of wrath.

"Fine, K.C.," his tone was cool, even icy. "If you think Pamela's so boring then why don't we talk about what *you* did today?" Father and Linda glanced over at me and I quickly realized my mistake.

"Oh, it was nothing, do go on about Pamela," I said weakly but it was too late.

"No, don't be shy, go on and tell them *all* about the things you saw," Rudy insisted grimly. "I think Father and Linda will be very interested to hear about what *you* consider a normal day." Father and Linda were waiting expectantly so I shrugged, offhandedly.

"Oh, it was nothing much. Just went and saw some stuff, is all." They exchanged glances as Rudy continued blithely.

"Be sure and mention about how you snooped around the construction site and saw a big thing come out of the water and —" here Rudy paused and smirked, "— melt into the cliff." I shot a dark look of reproach at him but he ignored it. "Well, you did," he added triumphantly. "You said so yourself."

"What's this?" Father turned a serious look on me.

"Well, for one thing, I *never* snoop," I informed them all with great dignity.

"Of course not," Linda nodded at me reassuringly, "you *investigate*, which is a different thing entirely." I gave her an appreciative look. Sometimes Linda's timing is excellent. Father and Rudy, on the other hand, were regarding me with identical, unwavering stares so I went on. "But as a matter of fact I did happen to see something weird."

"Like what?" Father wanted to know.

"Well, I was talking to Julian, near Ixchel's temple," I explained, eyeing Rudy defensively as he waggled his brows at me, "and when I looked down past the cliffs I saw a big, moving shape in the water down below."

"On the east side of the island?" Linda's eyes narrowed as I nodded. "But that's off limits to the public," she observed. "It's far too dangerous to even take a boat or anything out there. I know because I wanted to rent one to take a picture of the cliffs from below but Julian talked me out of it." I nodded eagerly at her.

"It wasn't even a boat, it was big and bulky, like a — I don't know. That's why it was so strange."

"Sometimes your eyes can play tricks on you, K.C. You might have mistaken a wave for something else," Father told me gently, using 'the voice of reason.' I sighed, folding my hands carefully on the table before me. "All right, assuming you saw a big shape," Father continued, trying to placate me, "then what?"

"Well, I walked along the coastline as far as I could to right below this construction site."

"The one behind the big screen?" Linda asked. "What are they building behind that thing anyway?" she wanted to know.

"It's just an ordinary cement block building, like a barn or something but without any windows. Ugly," I remarked.

"Oh."

"So did you see anything from the shore?" Father prompted and I resumed my story.

"Yeah, after a while I saw another dark shape sort of rise out of the water and melt into the cliff," I replied. "It wasn't a diver or anything like that either, it was just a big lump." The three of them regarded me patiently as though waiting for a punchline and I shrugged at them. "That's all."

"It just melted into the cliff?" Father repeated slowly and I nodded.

"That's right."

"It probably has something to do with the construction," Rudy put in, "wouldn't you think?"

"It might," Father admitted, "but all things considered I don't really think it's anything to be alarmed about, K.C." His tone was indulgent and I regarded him with mingled annoyance and affection.

Given the fact that he is a lawyer, I would have to say it's a good thing that Father evaluates situations logically, but sometimes I wish he would subscribe to the good old-fashioned mental process known as the 'intuitive leap.'

"But that's not all," Rudy prompted me curtly, "tell them all about Señor Colón's plot against you, too."

Father and Linda turned to me with looks of total dismay, and I gazed back somewhat apologetically.

"Well it's true you know, that guy who chased me the other day works for Señor Colón, and he saw me with

Julian at Chichén Itzá so it's only a matter of time before they find me."

"It is?" Linda asked weakly, her eyes wide with concern and I nodded.

"Billy Joe and Beau were there, at the construction site I mean, where I went walking today. It's built over the place in the cliff where the thing melted. Into the cliff, I mean." I took a deep breath and paused. My beloved family were unified in their looks of distress and as I watched they exchanged significant glances with each other.

Father cleared his throat. "I see." Sensing their disbelief I hastened to explain myself.

"Remember the statue?" A perplexed frown creased Linda's forehead.

"Yes, that *was* odd, wasn't it?" She was referring to the way Billy Joe had flatly denied the statue's existence. I leaned forward, including the three of them in my conspiratorial whisper.

"I think Billy Joe and Beau are planning to sell the statue or something. Maybe they even found a whole lot of artifacts in the ruins and are planning to smuggle them out of Mexico. They were talking about how they had to finish in two days because 'The Boss' is nervous about seeing me around. I think Señor Colón is the 'Boss' they're talking about, and remember, I saw him on the yacht with Billy Joe..." I slowed, then stopped talking, as I could tell from their expressions that I was not getting through.

Father, Linda and Rudy looked worried, but not quite in the way I had hoped. It was more the kind of look they might get if they were truly concerned for my sanity. "Really, I did hear them talking," I added weakly. There was silence while I stirred my ice cream. It had melted into a milky puddle during my lengthy recitation. Father regarded me uneasily and I thought I saw Linda give his hand a slight squeeze under the table.

"You don't believe me." I observed bluntly. "You think I'm going crazy." Father denied my words so quickly I knew they were true.

"It's not that we think you're going crazy, K.C., it's just that the doctors warned us that you might have —" he glanced at Linda,

"Lingering consequences from your experience in Vallarta," Linda finished. "It's quite common for veterans and prisoners of war or victims of an accident to go through a period where they think they're seeing things relating to their trauma." I shook my head in frustration.

"This is different, you have to believe me! Please!"

"We believe that you believe it honey, and that makes it real enough for us," Father assured me with deep compassion. I gave up my efforts to persuade them. "It might help if we all sit down and talk with someone," Father continued a little awkwardly. "We'll address your concerns and if there's a reason for alarm we'll take whatever steps are necessary to protect you."

Linda gave me a reassuring smile. "Don't feel bad, K.C., we'll get this whole thing all cleared up and everything will be fine." She was undoubtedly trying to comfort me but it sure wasn't working. I sat there for a moment, mulling it over. I could talk until I was twenty-one and they still wouldn't hear what I was saying.

"You know, I think maybe you're right after all. It's been a really long day, and I think I should get some rest." I passed a weary hand across my brow as Rudy straightened abruptly in his chair to watch me closely. Father and Linda both gave me relieved smiles.

Linda approved my plan. "Good idea, K.C., get some sleep and we'll all talk about it in the morning."

"Well, sleep well, sweetheart," Father said gently. "We'll be up later. Leave a light on for us so we don't crash around in the dark and wake you, all right?"

"Right, Later." I felt a little guilty about deceiving them all about the true reason for my early departure. After all, a person doesn't like to lie to her beloved family. On the other hand though, judging from their reaction to my story, I doubted that I would find much support from any of them for my early morning reconnaissance mission. In fact, I felt certain that if I had announced my plans, one or the other of them might have physically prevented me from going.

It wasn't so much that I didn't appreciate their concern for me. Father and Linda were obviously trying to act in my best interests (from their perspective of course), but I had a feeling that whatever Beau and Billy Joe were doing, they would be finishing up soon. From the way things were looking it seemed that by the time anyone took me seriously enough to look into this fishy business, it would be too late.

Surely there would be no harm if all I did was check out the construction site, look around a little and maybe take a few pictures of anything that looked suspicious. If I left early enough I'd be back before anyone even knew I was gone. And I might be a little closer to figuring out exactly what Billy Joe and Beau were up to.

Chapter Twelve

It was pitch-black when I awoke, and I grumbled quietly to myself as I got dressed without having showered. I left a note for Father on the living room table explaining that I was going out for a while and crept out the door of the apartment, latching it carefully behind me so I wouldn't disturb anyone.

The hotel was still asleep as I left and the streets were virtually deserted. Even the local birds were still snoozing and there was a creepy feeling in the heavy calm of the air. I ignored it and hurried a few blocks to the Restaurant Bar Gomar.

The place was utterly dark and quiet, and there was no sign of occupancy within. I hesitated then raised a fist and rapped loudly at the door. When this brought no response I knocked again, only louder. A moment later I heard a muffled exclamation from within.

A middle-aged woman opened the door. She was wearing a brightly colored caftan and a threatening glower which turned to surprised chagrin when she saw me standing there.

"¿Sí?" she eyed me dubiously, so I smiled and said, "I'm here for the golf cart rental. I spoke with your husband yesterday." The woman sighed and muttered something under her breath.

"*Sí, Sí*. Golf cart rental." Opening the door wider, she invited me in and preceded me to the desk where I filled out the obligatory paperwork for the rental contract. She watched me curiously as I paid the rest of the deposit, then filled in the blanks in the rental contract pertaining to my hotel, telephone and room number. I added Father's name in parentheses next to mine.

"*Mi padre,*" I explained, pointing and she nodded, a reluctant smile edging past her frown.

"*Está bien,*" she handed me the key and walked me outside to where the golf cart was parked. "*¿Dos horas?*" she reconfirmed our arrangement and I nodded, holding up two fingers.

"Two hours." I had the roads entirely to myself as I headed southeast toward the far end of the island. It was just me and the iguanas, but even the iguanas were few and far between. Apparently they had the sense to sleep past the first light of morning. It was unusually quiet, the air dense with moisture and an odd kind of heat enveloping me.

When I reached the open road running along the coast it was light, but not quite sunrise. I noticed that farther out to sea the sky was a threatening grey, as though a larger bank of clouds were about to roll inland. Since there was very little wind it was hard to tell whether they were headed toward or away from land so I decided to press on and turn back only if it looked like bad weather was imminent.

I reached the construction site without event and parked the cart carefully out of sight behind a thick clump of vegetation a few hundred yards down the road. I wasn't trying to hide my presence, exactly, but I didn't want anything to happen to the cart in my absence either.

I walked carefully through the patches of green vegetation and brush, heading for a spot above the path I'd followed the day before. I figured if I were careful, I could watch the construction site from the side rather than approach it from the road. That way I'd be able to keep an eye on the door.

I could only hope that I'd be able to find a good hiding spot before anyone saw me there, as it would be kind of hard to explain my presence on the cliffs for two days in a row as accidental, especially since I'd already been informed that it was private property.

I didn't actually have much of a plan other than to watch and see who, if anyone, came and went from the big building. If my theory was right, then there would be no one around except Billy Joe and Beau, who were working 'overtime.' I planned to give it about two hours, maybe go in for a closer look then return to the hotel in time for breakfast with no one the wiser to my scheme.

I settled down in the shadow of the boulder at the cliff's edge and checked to see that I had remembered to load my little camera with a fresh roll of film. It was unlikely that I would see anything worth photographing at this hour, but just in case I needed it, my camera was ready.

The small parking lot was easily visible behind the building, and I could see Beau's truck parked there. Evidently, I was not the only one to get an early start on the day. I took a long drink from my water bottle before recapping it, then checked my watch.

I must have waited there for about fifteen minutes before I saw anything at all. Billy Joe emerged from the double doors at the front of the concrete structure and glanced around, taking a long pull of his cigarette before tossing it into the dust at his feet.

He looked like he hadn't shaved for a long time and as I watched he turned to call to someone over his shoulder. Beau joined him and the two men talked for a moment, then separated. Billy Joe crossed the dirt-paved parking area and started the pickup truck, while Beau disappeared into the storage facility.

Billy Joe smoked another entire cigarette while he idled the truck and eventually Beau left the facility and climbed into the truck beside Billy Joe. They talked for a minute, then Billy Joe gunned the engine and they disappeared in a cloud of dust. I waited for another thirty minutes, just watching the door to the facility and pondering the likelihood that they would return.

Finally the temptation was too great. I got up, brushed myself off and tiptoed toward the building itself. I justified my actions by promising myself that it wouldn't really be 'breaking and entering' since I wouldn't be breaking anything, I'd just be looking. The building was unlocked, and when I tried the door it opened easily at my touch. I hesitated, looked around to make certain I wasn't being observed, then went inside, my heart pounding with the adrenaline rush of taking that forbidden step.

The inside of the building was unremarkable. Dull, even. There were a few rows of empty metal shelving, stretching from ceiling to floor with nothing at all on them, a collection of work tools consistent with carpentry, and little else. I headed farther back into the building, my footsteps as quiet as I could make them on the concrete floor.

I walked all the way to the back, to the side closest to the parking lot, but still found nothing. It was much darker back here. There were no windows at all and the entire area was barely lit by a chaotic string of bulbs hanging on hooks overhead.

The sound of muffled voices reached my ears just then and I broke into a panicked sprint for the door, thinking that maybe Beau and Billy Joe had returned. I hoped to reach the safety of the bushes before they could park the truck and round the building. When I ran outside however, there was no sign of either of them.

Not only that, but I could no longer even hear the voices once I had left the building. That gave me food for thought, and I raced for my hiding place by the boulder, determined to find a safe spot before considering matters any further. And I was glad I did, for not thirty seconds after I had crouched behind the big rock a man came out of the building and strode briskly toward the parking lot, carrying an oddly-shaped package under his arm.

I watched as another man emerged from the building and jogged after him, calling and waving to attract the first man's attention. The first one waited for him and then the two of them walked toward the road, laughing and talking until they were out of sight. A minute later I heard a car's engine being started, and once the sound faded away I stood up again, regarding the facility with a puzzled frown.

Now, I knew full well that there had been no one else inside the building when I'd been in there. Nor were there any doors other than the one I had used. So where had the two men come from?

I hesitated, looking out to sea, and realized that during my brief time inside the sky had darkened considerably. A brisk wind had picked up and was blowing toward me from across the water. It carried the faint odor of ozone and I shivered, for it was obvious that a storm was heading inland. The way things looked, I wouldn't have much time to get back to the hotel before the rain came.

I had to move fast. I decided to go back inside one more time to see if I could at least figure out how those two men had gotten inside without my noticing.

Then, I promised myself, I would leave, return the golf cart and go have a normal breakfast with my family. Boy, was I ever wrong about that last part. I hid my water bottle and notebook under a bush by the boulder, and headed briskly toward the facility.

I opened the door with caution and peered inside. The two men who had just left had evidently turned out the lights behind them because the place was in darkness. I groped for a light switch on the wall by the door but it was nowhere to be found.

I hesitated, holding the door open a little way while my eyes adjusted to the dimness of the interior, then I closed it behind me. I should have been in total darkness but to my surprise there was a gentle glow to my left, behind a row of shelves. I tiptoed toward it.

To my amazement I saw a wide-open trap door with what looked like metal stairs leading down. The source of the light was apparently a set of small spotlights inside the mysterious stairway below the floor.

I crept noiselessly toward the trap door, curiosity overriding common sense, and looked down into a tunnel leading steeply down into the cliff wall. I froze there, my mind reeling, trying to grasp the implications of what I saw.

My first, frightened thought was to leave immediately but I didn't have that option really, for it was then I heard Billy Joe and Beau, who had now returned. My only warning of their arrival was the loud slam of car doors.

I glanced around in panic. It was too late to leave the building, and even if I did make it outside they would surely see me running away. I thought of hiding behind a row of shelves but it just wouldn't work, there simply wasn't enough cover to pull it off. There was no place to go but down, so down I went.

The stairs were made of reinforced steel and as I scrambled hastily downward I noticed a conveyer belt running parallel to the stairs, right up to the floor of the storage facility. I didn't have time to really study the set-up though, if you know what I mean. I heard the door crash open upstairs and Billy Joe's voice echoing through the facility.

"Let's finish it up," he was saying, as two sets of footsteps pounded across the floor toward the trap door. I looked around at my options. What I was hoping for was a closet or some place where I could hide until they left. What I saw was just more tunnel, sloping smoothly downward until it curved away to the left. I had no choice but to follow it.

The limestone stairs were smooth and damp underfoot and I went forward as quickly as I dared, rounding the curve at a run. The tunnel was only about twenty feet long but it felt like a mile, and when I reached the end I was amazed to see that it widened out into a series of natural caves, just like the cave with the underground pool where I'd swum near Chichén Itzá.

The caves were lit up by the same kind of crude spotlights as I had seen inside the building above. The effect was quite eery.

I noticed that there were three smaller tunnels leading from the left wall of the main cave and I hid around the corner of the middle one, clinging to the cold wall and trying to breathe quietly. (Which is really hard to do when you're panicking).

I hid just in time, too, for Billy Joe and Beau followed out not five seconds later, laughing and talking.

"...conveyor belt fixed so we can start shipping the stuff out," Beau finished his sentence. I stopped breathing entirely as the two of them walked right past my hiding place. To my intense relief, they never noticed me there but kept right on walking, their voices fading rapidly into the echoing space of the largest cave.

I thought about my options. Part of me wanted to return to the trap door, leave the building and go back to the hotel. I knew that neither Father nor Linda would believe me when I told them what I had seen. More likely, they would send for a doctor to examine me. I finally decided that since I wasn't in any immediate danger, I might as well see what I could see, take a few pictures, then leave.

I tiptoed back out into the largest cave, took a quick photo then followed the same path leading downward that Billy Joe and Beau had taken. It was evident that someone had taken pains to make the walkway traversable. The stone path was smooth and even. It had been carved out of the rock itself and was a uniform four feet wide most of the way down.

To the right side of the path was a flat rubber conveyor belt which was supported by sturdy steel-jointed scaffolding. The path curved abruptly to the left. I paused for a moment to listen and found that I could hear the sea. I could also hear the clanking grind of machinery, and a kind of diesel hum too, both barely audible over the sound of the waves.

I looked around the corner and found myself at the top of a steel stairway leading down to the floor of an even bigger cave. Its massive stone walls arched upward to a jagged ceiling, while the outer walls, closest to the sea, narrowed to a thin, vertical 'V' opening in the cliff. A movement below suddenly caught my eye. Beau and Billy Joe walked out from under the stairs beneath me. They were deep in conversation, and didn't see me. I ducked back around the corner again, out of sight.

Chapter Thirteen

When I was sure I hadn't been noticed, I crouched low to the stone floor and peeked around the corner at them.

Billy Joe and Beau were now working below me on the rocky floor of the cave, operating a hydraulic hoist underneath what looked like a waterlogged crate. The crate hung above them from a metal clamp on a thick steel cable running from the back of the cave out to the sea. The near end of the cable was attached to the wall about twenty feet from where I was hiding and I studied it curiously.

There was a sudden whining noise around me and I flinched, looking for the source of the sound. It came from the cable motor assembly on the wall, its meshing gears straining to force the cable around two massive pulley heads also bolted to the cave wall. As I watched, the cable slackened abruptly and when I looked down, I saw that Beau and Billy Joe had successfully unloaded the crate.

The crate was now on the hoist's forked lift. Billy Joe lowered it slowly, turning the hoist as he did so in order to load the crate onto the conveyor belt. The conveyor belt began creaking and groaning as it slowly moved the heavy load upwards toward my hiding spot. I watched silently as Beau retrieved a cell phone from his pocket, punched in a number then had a terse conversation with someone.

I fumbled in my pocket for my camera and squeezed off a flashless shot of Billy Joe, Beau and the crate as it slowly passed by. Just one picture for the record — that way Rudy and Father would have to believe me when I told them what I'd seen.

I was still holding the camera when I heard footsteps approaching me. There was no place for me to hide even if I'd had time to try, and I confess I froze in place, listening with apprehension as the person unknown approached me. My terror turned to weak relief when I saw Julian standing there looking down at me with an expression of shocked disbelief.

"K.C.?" he sounded utterly astonished, "is that you?"

"Julian! Man am I glad to see you!" I whispered, beckoning him toward my hiding spot. "You have to see this, Billy Joe and Beau are smuggling something down there, they're —" I slowed and came to a stop, staring at Julian in growing horror. When I stopped to think about it, I couldn't help noticing that he looked right at home there in the cave. He met my eyes briefly then glanced away, his shoulders slumping.

"You're in on it too, aren't you. You probably made all that up about the statue," I whimpered, a sick numb feeling spreading through my stomach. As I watched, a dull red flush crept up from under Julian's collar.

"Get up and give me the camera," he ordered me quietly. I got to my feet slowly, handing it over as Julian turned to shout, "Beau! Billy Joe!" I was too stunned by Julian's betrayal to even protest when he ushered me down the stairway toward his partners.

Beau and Billy Joe had paused in their labors as we joined them and I got the distinct impression that they were not at all pleased to see me standing there.

"Where did you find her?" Beau asked Julian.

"Right up there," Julian turned to look at me but I couldn't bear to meet his eyes as he handed my camera to Beau, who scowled down at it darkly, turning it over and over in his hands.

"I'm sorry, I was just looking around," I mumbled. "Are you guys reconstructing the ruins from inside the cliff or something?" I was going for the naive approach and Beau's eyes flickered.

"Yeah, that's what we're doing all right," he replied offhandedly, fingering my camera with idle contempt before dropping it to the stone at his feet. "Oops, sorry kid." So saying, Beau stomped my camera to death beneath his work boot. An ominous rumble of thunder lent uncanny emphasis to his gesture.

I opened my mouth to protest Beau's action, then snapped it shut quickly, glancing in quick protest at Julian before I remembered that he was one of them. He caught my look and flushed.

"Listen, K.C.," he had to speak up in order to make himself heard over the growing wind, "I can't really explain all this to you but you really aren't in any danger, as long as you do what we say." Billy Joe coughed loudly at these words. "Now, how about it?"

"How about what?" I tilted my chin at him. "What do you mean? Are you saying you're going to keep me here until you're finished then let me go?"

"I'm sorry, K.C., that's the deal," Julian nodded wearily.

"Oh come on, man," Beau put in derisively. "That's not a solution." I watched him warily, hoping he didn't mean what I thought he meant. He did though. "Let's just get rid of her now and get back to work, no sense in wastin' time on it," Beau suggested matter-of-factly. A violent flash of lightning split the sky, now turning black with churning clouds. Julian shook his head.

"No. That's not an option. It would be stupid to add murder to everything else." Julian sounded calm, but I could see he was clenching and unclenching his hands in his pockets. "I mean, look at her, she's just a little kid," he shrugged dismissively. But Beau shook his head, and the howling wind ruffled his thick blonde hair as he regarded me through slitted eyes.

"She's a very tricky little kid, that's what she is. She had a camera on her, man, I'm telling you she probably took pictures and everything. I'm sorry, man, but she's gotta go." Beau reached inside his pocket and calmly pulled out a gun the way most people pull out a wallet, without even looking. I gulped.

"Don't," Julian said, white-faced, putting up a hand to stop him.

"Why not?" A crunching sound interrupted this cheery little debate and Beau whipped around, his mouth working oddly as he saw another crate appear not far from the mouth of the cave. It was swinging wildly back and forth in the wind, and as we watched a strong gust of wind slammed it splinteringly hard into the rock near the cave mouth.

"What are those idiots doing? Don't they know it's storming up here on the surface?"

Beau glanced up at the cable which was shivering and twisting in the wind. "Cut the power," he yelled furiously to Billy Joe. "No, don't, it's too late! Just get it inside!" Billy Joe sprinted for the mouth of the cave, and picked up a long metal pole with a hook on one end.

The crate swung wildly back and forth in the gale outside, and I could see Billy Joe cursing a mile a minute as he wielded the pole, desperately trying to guide the crate safely inside the cave. He was soon drenched from head to toe by a thick, salty spray from the waves below.

"I'll watch the girl, go help Billy Joe!" Julian shouted to Beau and I realized quite suddenly that they had to shout in order to make themselves heard over the howling of the wind. Beau looked from me to Julian and then shook his head, shouting back.

"Not a chance! I'll watch the girl and *you* go help him!" Beau shifted the gun slightly in his palm, as if to remind Julian that he was still holding it and I saw Julian's eyes narrow slightly. With a last backward look at me he strode rapidly across the cave floor to assist Billy Joe in his attempts to save the dangling crate.

Beau kept a watchful eye on me as Billy Joe and Julian did their best to steer the crate safely inside the cave, but their efforts were doomed. A gust of wind caught it, slamming it viciously against one side of the mouth of the cave. With a resounding crack one side of the crate broke open, and out spilled what looked like old metal objects. I caught a glimmer of silver in the jumble on the floor.

Billy Joe and Julian began scooping the contents of the crate away from the cave mouth, fighting the wind, while Beau looked from them, to me, then back to them impatiently. I could tell that I had suddenly become a nuisance. Finally Beau seemed to make up his mind and strode forward to seize me, pushing me roughly toward the opening.

"Hey!" I shouted and fought desperately when he seized my arm. "Let go!"

"What are you doing?" Julian heard my shout and abandoned his efforts to interpose himself between Beau and me.

"We don't have time to be messing around with witnesses!" Beau shouted, glaring at me over Julian's shoulder.

Julian tried to stop him. "It's too risky! If you shoot her, they'll come looking around, and we can't afford that kind of trouble. Not now!"

"I'm not going to shoot her."

"What?"

"I said, I'm not going to shoot her!" Beau shouted again, louder. He jerked his head in the direction of the cave mouth. "She's going to have an accident!" I stared at them both with disbelief. My day had just gone from bad to worst ever.

"Julian," I whispered the word but he seemed to hear me. His face twisted and he shouted:

"No!" He stepped closer to block Beau. Beau looked at him consideringly for a moment while, off to one side, Billy Joe paused in his labors and watched this scene with a look of impatience.

"Just waste the kid man, we gotta get back to work!" Billy Joe screamed against the wind.

"Let's go, kid." Beau stepped around Julian and gestured with the gun, indicating that I should move up to the mouth of the cave. I didn't budge. "You're going out there one way or another, kid, bullet or not. Now you decide," Beau told me coldly. Then, without a word, Julian launched himself at Beau, tackling him from the side.

Staggering sideways, Beau went down and for a moment it looked like Julian was going to succeed as he fought for the gun in Beau's hand.

Then Billy Joe entered the fray. Using the long metal pole he held as a weapon, he swung it two-handed at Julian, catching him in the shoulders and toppling him from where he was still trying to force the gun from Beau's fingers. Billy Joe wielded the pole again, this time connecting solidly with Julian's head and Julian went down in a heap on the cold stone floor. It happened too fast for me to help him, even if I'd had the means to do so. Beau stood up, his face livid with anger, and raised the gun, pointing it straight at me.

"OK, OK, I'm going!" I shouted, stalling for time. I looked around desperately as I backed toward the mouth of the cave. I knew for sure that if I didn't do something, *anything*, I would die. There was no weapon with which I could fight back, and no time to search for one.

Out of the corner of my eye I saw Julian stir slightly then rise slowly to his feet. The steel cable twanged weirdly in the wind above my head and I glanced up at it briefly, studying the shattered wreckage of the crate dangling there while a sort of plan formed in my head. I glanced back at Beau and knew from the look in his eyes that he was about to pull the trigger so I said a prayer to Ixchel and got a running start on the mouth of the cave.

A bullet zinged past my head as I leaped like a hurdler, jumping up to desperately grab at the remains of the broken crate hanging there.

Chapter Fourteen

It was a weird moment when my feet left the cave floor and I knew there was no turning back. I had hoped to grab the crate and use it to slide down the cable, out of range of Beau and his gun. That's not what happened, though.

The crate, already savaged by its encounter with the walls of the cave, proved unequal to the test of my weight and tore loose from its attachment to the cable with me hanging on for dear life as I fell into the churning water below. It was only about a thirty foot drop but it felt like a mile and I screamed like a baby the whole way down.

I landed on the side of a huge wave which whirled me up one side of its heaving crest and down the other side as I struggled and fought to hold onto my only friend, the smashed wooden crate, riding it as though I were whitewater rafting. Another wave hurled me toward the cliff. Then I found myself at the very top of a wall of water, falling straight down, and I was conscious of a dull pain in my right leg.

For a moment everything was swirling water and blackness while my makeshift raft and I were tossed like a load of dirty laundry. Then another wave lifted me up back out to sea. It felt like I was caught in a strange dance with two opposing partners, each one pulling a different way. I swallowed sea water, but managed to hold onto the crate.

When my head was above water I looked around, trying to get my bearings. I could see a dim glow from the cave above and far off to my right. Somehow, I had been swept more than a hundred yards from the point where I'd first landed. For the first time a small ray of hope beamed in me.

The wind was strong, coming from the northeast. It was blowing straight at the southeastern end of the island. If I could manage to stay afloat long enough for the current to pull me around the tip of Isla Mujeres, I might have a chance in the quieter waters on the other side.

My right leg felt heavy and useless. I could tell it had been hurt. Every time another wave dunked me and the crate I had more and more trouble holding on. At one point it did occur to me that I was not going to make it, but I didn't let that stop me from trying.

About the time that I could no longer see the light from the cave above me I rounded the tip of the island. The wind slackened slightly and I could see the lights of Cancún across the bay, and more lights from down the coast to my right, probably from Garrafón beach.

I clung to the splintered crate and kicked desperately for shore, fighting the pull of the current which would have carried me farther toward Cancún. Luckily for me, the waves were much smaller in the shallow water of the southwest side of the island.

I felt an uncomfortable scraping sensation as the waves flung me down onto a coral reef, then I felt myself being sucked into a strong current heading for shore. I thanked my lucky stars, right up until I landed hard on a rock.

I clung there for dear life, waiting for the wave to recede and when it had I staggered onto the shore, dripping and shivering with exhaustion and relief as I fell down on the sand. I lay there spread-eagled for a while, until I had coughed most of the water from my lungs, then sat up. The shattered crate bobbed sluggishly in the shallow water nearby, a mere remnant of what it had once been. I knew that without it I would have been the one pounded to splinters on the rocks.

The sky above was no longer churning black. At first I thought I was imagining things, but then I realized that the storm was finally passing. The swollen black clouds had blown past Isla Mujeres and were hanging across the bay, directly over Cancún.

It was an awesome sight. The twinkling lights of the luxury hotels were nearly extinguished by the black clouds and rain besieging them. I could still hear the crack and sizzle of lightning but the noise of the thunder following it was fading. A hard rain was still falling though, and I felt cold and tired, and very alone.

The throbbing in my leg was pretty awful and when I checked, I was appalled to see that I had a four-inch bleeding gash on my right thigh. My immersion in the cold water had slowed the bleeding to a trickle though, and when I tried I found I could still stand.

I limped and hopped through the rough underbrush which bordered the rocky beaches of Garrafón National Park. I was stunned and thinking only of getting to the road where I might be able to flag down some help.

I had just reached the last incline and was heading through the thick brush toward the asphalt about a hundred yards away when I saw, to my relief, a police car coming along the road.

I lurched forward, feebly shouting, "Help!" and trying to windmill my arms as it neared me, but it passed by, the driver amazingly unaware of my presence. To my intense frustration I also saw Father sitting in the rear passenger seat, but he was looking at the road ahead, not to the side where I was. Then the car was gone, — just taillights fading into the grey twilight of the storm's aftermath. D-a-d-d-y!

I stood in the middle of the road for a moment then set out on foot after the police car, trudging damply through the muck. The rain had left quite a mess in its wake; the road, which had been dusty the day before, was now a swirling mess of mud, and my feet squelched thickly in it.

I walked about a hundred yards then sat down to rest. My head was aching fiercely and I was shivering so hard my teeth were chattering. My right leg throbbed with a slow hot ache and I was starting to wonder if I'd be able to walk anymore when I heard another car coming from the direction in which police car had disappeared.

I stood hopefully by the road, but when the car rounded the hilltop I could see it wasn't the police car at all, just an ordinary jeep. The car slowed, then stopped. The driver was watching me with an alarmed expression.

"*Por favor.*" I limped over to the car as he got out. It was the same young man who'd warned me away from the cliff. At the sight of my waterlogged appearance and bloody leg he broke into a torrent of Spanish, obviously questioning me about what had happened.

I shook my head wearily and he stooped to examine my leg. After a moment he turned away without a word to rummage around in the back seat of the jeep and returned with a roll of electrical tape and a rag.

I held still while he bound the rag tightly in place over the gash with tape. When he had finished binding my leg he poked at my shoulder gently, sending a wave of stinging pain across it. I yelped in surprise, looking down to where he'd touched me.

I'd forgotten my encounter with the coral reef. My shirt hung in ribbons across my shoulder and left arm from when I'd been flung by a wave against the reef, and my skin had been scored by a series of stinging welts. The man gave me a thoughtful look then opened the passenger door of the car, indicating that I should get in.

I hesitated then complied, thinking that he would drive me into town and to the hospital. To my surprise, he turned the car around and headed back toward Ixchel's Temple and the neighboring construction site.

I wrenched at the door of the jeep, intending to fling myself out and make a run for it, but then I saw the police car parked up ahead, and Father standing beside it with two other officers in uniform. They were apparently having a discussion of some kind with Billy Joe, who was standing defensively in front of the door leading into the facility. There was no sign of Julian or Beau.

When my driver saw that I was intending to jump from the moving vehicle he hit the brakes, and the combination of this plus the fact that I had already managed to open the door part way sent me flying out of the jeep where I sprawled in the mud about fifty yards from my father, the wind knocked completely out of me.

"¡Señorita!" Obviously shocked at the results of his attempt to save me from harm, the young man hurried

around the front of the jeep to help me to my feet. "*¿La señorita está OK?*" I nodded at him, shivering violently.

"I'm fine, thanks," I assured him, wincing, once I could speak again. He hoisted me up and without another word I limped off toward the police car. I had a word or two I wanted to add to whatever Father was saying to Billy Joe.

Oddly enough, no one had noticed me yet, as they were standing in a tense little circle near the door, staring at one another while they talked. As I drew nearer, I could see that Father was holding the plastic water bottle I'd left behind in my hiding place near the boulder.

"She must have been here!" He spoke in an extremely clipped tone, the way he does when he's very, very angry. "Now listen here, this is K.C.'s water bottle. Are you trying to tell me you never saw her here?" Billy Joe glanced dispassionately from the bottle to the faces of the two policemen.

"So your kid left her bottle here. That don't mean anything, she could have left it at some other time. I'm telling you nobody here has seen her."

"*Señorita,*" the driver of the jeep was hurrying after me, and at the sound of his voice Billy Joe glanced in our direction. His face went dead white when he saw me there and I smiled at him fiercely, enjoying the look of absolute shock on his face.

"Well, hi there, Billy Joe," I called as I drew near. "Y'all remember me?" At the sound of my voice Father whirled around and stared at me in puzzled confusion. Just then, Linda and Rudy came running up to us and I saw the same confusion mixed with relief on their faces. I guessed that in my current state I was a little hard to recognize.

Chapter Fifteen

"K.C., are you all right?" With a gasp, Linda flew to me, her eyes shining with relief. "My God, James, just look at her! Sweetie, what happened to you?" Rudy quietly crossed the distance between us and stood protectively at my side.

"Be careful," I directed my remark to the officers standing there watching us in bemusement. "He probably has a gun." I looked straight at Billy Joe as I said this and he half turned away from us, as though he were intending to open the door behind him.

"Not so fast, Señor." One of the officers put up a hand to stop him while the other casually patted him down and, finding no weapon, stepped back.

"K.C., what happened to you?" Father started to hug me but stopped when I winced. Gently he examined my shoulder, his look changing from one of concern to anger. I saw a muscle jump in his jaw when he noticed my leg.

"Beau and Billy Joe made me jump into the sea from the cave during the storm. Julian tried to stop them but they beat him up." My teeth were still chattering and Rudy removed his jacket to drape it gently around me.

"Here," he said simply, "you want to sit down?"

"No thanks," I shook my head, still looking at the two police officers. "You should arrest him," I told them both, pointing at Billy Joe. "He and Beau tried to kill me because I found out what's going on in the cave." Billy Joe had recovered somewhat from the shock of seeing me and shrugged, feigning unconcern.

"Cave? There's no cave. The kid probably hit her head on a rock. She's hallucinating."

"There is too a cave!" I retorted, furiously. "Don't lie, you big jerk, you were right there!"

"What cave?" Linda interjected gently. "K.C., tell us what cave?"

"There's a cave in the cliffs, you can't see it from here but Beau and Billy Joe and Julian are using it to stash something they're bringing up on a cable from the sea," I insisted.

The two police officers exchanged uncomfortable glances and I could tell that they were finding my story a little implausible. After all, they had probably known Billy Joe for some time while I, on the other hand, was a distraught little girl, leveling absurd and unfounded accusations.

"See what I mean? The kid has a concussion. She's seeing things." Billy Joe dismissed my story with an offhand wave and Rudy winced at this choice of words. "Now, if you don't mind, I need to get on with my work. You've found the kid and I don't see as how there's any more reason for you to be here."

"Ask him why he's here instead of at work on the ruins," I said to Father. I was trembling with rage at Billy Joe's attempt to just walk away from what he'd done.

"That's a good question," Father said, "What about that?" Billy Joe shrugged and rolled his eyes at the policemen who were looking at us with the tolerance of movie goers watching the final credits. The show was over, they'd found the lost *turista*, and now it was time to go home.

"I just came over to see what kind of damage the storm had done. I was just looking around," he replied.

"Make him let you look inside the storage building. There's a trap door in the floor which leads to a tunnel to the cave," I persisted. Now the policemen eyed me uncertainly.

"I'd like to speak to Julian Sayles at once," Father addressed them both crisply. "He's the one in charge and he can get to the bottom of this." There was a moment's pause then the two officers shrugged and nodded, agreeing that it was a good idea. The first one turned to Billy Joe politely.

"Where is Señor Sayles, Señor Walton?"

"I'm sorry but he's not available right now," Billy Joe replied smoothly. "He's very busy."

"Liar!" I snapped, suddenly furious again. "I'll bet he's still right down there in the cave, you and Beau probably killed him the way you tried to kill me!" Even Billy Joe looked a little taken aback by my outburst.

"I believe K.C. I think she's telling the truth," Rudy said firmly and I looked up at him in total surprise as he continued, "She may be a Kook Case, but she's no liar."

"James," Linda agreed, "there really is something odd going on here. I think we should take a look inside the building, like K.C. says."

"I think so too," Father replied grimly, "so how about it?" Billy Joe shook his head.

"This here is private property and that means no trespassing, no way, no sir." His lips thinned slightly as he appealed to the now-confused police officers: "Listen, *amigos,* this is all just some kind of mixup. The kid is just probably concussed or something, she looks pretty beat up. Must have slipped on the rocks and fallen down the cliff. Look, I'll have Señor Sayles give you a call as soon as he returns, he'll get this whole thing straightened out."

The police officers looked at each other and shrugged again. It was plain that they had no wish to make an issue of things and force their way inside a site clearly marked "private property" on nothing more than the word of one slightly hysterical and moderately banged-up little girl.

"Perhaps that would be best," one of the officers agreed, looking at Father apologetically. Billy Joe gave me a gloating look and I stared back at him in fury then turned abruptly away, limping as fast as I could toward the boulder I'd hidden behind earlier. Rudy ran after me, concerned.

"K.C., where are you going?" I glanced back to see them all staring after me and Billy Joe's expression grew distinctly anxious as I leaned against the boulder, looking down along the cliffs toward where I knew the cave to be. My timing was perfect.

"There!" I waved and pointed triumphantly. "Look, you can see it!"

"It's true, she's right!" Rudy shouted excitedly. "There's something down there!" Father and Linda hurried over, closely followed by one of the police officers.

They were all in time to see a crate rise from the sea on a cable, float upward through the air, and then disappear inside the cave. Apparently operations below were back to normal since the storm had subsided.

"*¡Madre de Diós!*" the policeman whistled, watching in astonishment for a moment before rejoining his partner. Billy Joe looked uneasily from one policeman to the other, then started backing away slowly toward the parking lot.

"He's getting away!" I shouted and the officers whirled to see Billy Joe running for the parking lot. Billy Joe managed to run fast, even through the mud, but he wasn't fast enough. Sprinting toward him like a cougar, Rudy brought him down in a stunning tackle, leaping at him from six feet away and slamming him to the ground in a truly dramatic way. Sometimes it pays to have an older brother who excels at sports.

"Where do you think you're going, scum-bucket?" Rudy growled, pinning Billy Joe to the ground until the policemen reached his side. "Keep an eye on him," Rudy admonished the officer who handcuffed Billy Joe, "he's a mean little —" he caught Father's eye on him and finished weakly, "—son of a gun." Rudy stood back, allowing them to haul Billy Joe roughly to his feet. He brushed himself off and growled at Rudy.

"That's assault, kid, I hope you have a good attorney."

"You better believe he does," Father assured him smoothly. "Me." Billy Joe licked his lips nervously at these words and one of the officers spoke.

"You are not going anywhere right now, Señor Walton. You will stay right here and answer questions while we find Señor Sayles." He opened the driver's side door of the police car and made radio contact with someone, presumably calling for backup and I felt a wave of relief as the other officer drew his gun and opened the door to the storage facility.

"Why don't you show us what you have found, señorita," he invited me, "that is if you can make it?" Rudy wrapped a protective arm around my shoulder.

"It's OK if you need to lean a little," he murmured and I nodded at the policeman.

"I can make it," I muttered as we passed into the facility. "It's right there." I pointed past two recently-arrived wooden crates, still wet from their trip through the sea, to the open trap door. "Now we have to be careful because Beau is down here, and I know he has a gun." Rudy's arm tightened around my shoulder as we lurched down the stairs after the officer, closely followed by Father and Linda. I gasped in pain.

"Sorry," Rudy muttered, easing a bit.

The officer led the way cautiously into the tunnel below, from where I indicated the way to the main cave. I couldn't help noticing my companions' expressions change from curiosity to sheer wonder at the sight of the place we had entered.

"It might have been used by Spanish pirates long ago. How perfect," Linda whispered. "Can't you just see it, James?" Father nodded distractedly over his shoulder, following the officer closely.

"It's up ahead," I warned him in a low voice and we all walked along as quietly as we could past the conveyor belt and down the wide stone path to the top of the stairs. Mindful of my advice, the policeman peered around the corner cautiously.

"Billy Joe?" Beau's voice floated up to us. "That you?"

"That's Beau," I whispered softly. "He's the one who's armed." The officer nodded, his eyes intent as he walked out onto the stairs, his gun drawn and held steadily in both hands.

"Señor!" he shouted, "Yes, you! I am Officer Hidalgo and this is official police business. Put your hands in the air and stay very still." There was silence and then Officer Hidalgo started walking down the stairs, Father and Linda close on his heels. Rudy fairly carried me down two steps at a time in order not to miss any of the action.

"Ouch!" I yelped as he swung me down to the ground, depositing me behind Father.

"Sorry," Rudy apologized again.

Beau was standing near the mouth of the cave, a long steel pole in his hands. A large, waterlogged crate hung over his head and it was clear that he had been working alone, trying to guide the crate into position over the hoist, in order to unload it.

Officer Hidalgo patted him down, removed Beau's gun from his pocket, and cuffed his hands behind his back just as his partner joined us from above, accompanied by yet another officer. Backup officers had apparently arrived. Beau stared unbelievingly at me as I walked over to face him.

"You?" his eyes looked a little wild.

"Me," I nodded. "Where's Julian? You might as well tell us, you know." Beau snapped something unprintable at me and the policeman jerked his hand-cuffed arms roughly up behind him. Beau lapsed into silence quite suddenly.

"Where is Señor Sayles?" Officer Hidalgo repeated with very firm politeness, all the while tightening his grip. Beau blinked in pain, sweat beaded his upper lip and I thought I even saw a quick shimmer of tears in his eyes. Served him right.

"Over there." Beau jerked his head sullenly toward the back of the cave.

"Keep him here," Hidalgo told his partner who nodded and drew his gun as Hidalgo strode rapidly toward the back of the cave with Rudy and I hobbling after him.

He paused back there, leaned over, then disappeared from sight behind several oil drums stored there. A moment later he was helping someone to his feet and I recognized Julian, battered though he was.

"Julian?" I called anxiously, "are you OK?" Actually, Julian was noticeably *not* OK. In fact he was limping, rubbing his wrists and it looked as though he had been tied up and lying on the floor. One side of him was all muddy. At least he was alive. He looked up at my words and despite some nasty bruising his face lit up with a smile as the officer escorted him toward us.

"K.C.? You made it!" His knees buckled suddenly and he would have fallen except that the officer put a strong arm under him. "Thank God you're alive," he added fervently as they drew nearer.

"Julian," Beau spoke up suddenly, desperately, "tell them we don't have anything to do with any of this. Tell them the truth, how we found this cave right after the storm." Julian paused, swaying, to give Beau a look of utter contempt.

"The truth. Yeah, you're right, it is time for the truth," he replied bitterly. "It'll be a refreshing change." Beau's face whitened at these words and Julian turned away, beckoning to Officer Hidalgo. "Come here and take a look inside this crate." Julian walked with determination over to the hoist and raised it, expertly handlling the crate.

"Don't do that, man!" Beau protested, then subsided into silence as the officer nearest him turned to give him a furious look.

"Throw that switch," Julian instructed Father and I pointed to the switch nailed to the wall where he was standing. Father flipped the switch. The crate, which must have been clamped to the cable by some kind of magnet, dropped neatly onto the hoist and Julian lowered it gently to the floor of the cave. With a crowbar he pried the top off and stood back, inviting the others to take a look.

Officer Hidalgo went over to investigate. He reached into the box and pulled out a small metal object which glinted gold in the light. He held it up, turning it this way and that while Linda crossed the cave to study the contents of the box as well.

"My God, James, it's full of Spanish artifacts. There are old coins and jewels. I think I even see some knives and forks in here. This has to be hundreds of years old. Why —" she turned to the rest of us, her face flushed with excitement, "—this is probably from the first of the Spanish Conquistadors!"

Chapter Sixteen

"It's from the wreck of a ship belonging to Francisco Roberto Regalado, actually," Julian put in dryly, a faint smile twisting his lips.

"Who?" Linda scowled at him blankly.

"He was a Spanish merchant-pirate who shipwrecked here on Isla Mujeres almost five hundred years ago, in 1508." Linda gasped.

"Are you sure?"

Julian nodded. "I found records of the ship's inventory in Madrid. Regalado was a wealthy trader who, it seemed, went missing on a voyage in 1508, his whereabouts unknown. He might have died in the wreck, or he could have survived and lived here on the island." Linda got slowly to her feet.

"But you know what this means, right?" She could barely contain her excitement and Julian nodded sadly.

"Believe me, I do."

"What?" I, for one, was willing to be enlightened.

"It means that Francisco Hernández de Cordova was *not* the first person to discover the Yucatán peninsula. He didn't get here until 1517."

"That's right," Julian nodded, "it was old Regalado all along."

"But this is an amazing discovery. Julian, why didn't you tell anyone you'd found the wreck?" Linda asked him. "You'd be a legend in your own time!" Her face fell abruptly as she realized her error. "Oh, er... yes, right," she stammered, glancing from Beau to Julian, now at a loss for words.

"A legend!" Beau laughed rudely and Julian flushed bright red. "Yeah, Mr. Big-Shot Sayles, go ahead and tell the police why you didn't announce your big discovery." Beau's tone was so contemptuous that we all looked at him in surprise. Even more surprising was Julian's embarrassed reaction.

"It was a few years ago," he glanced at all of us then away, his lips twisted self-deprecatingly. "I was younger, you know? I couldn't get any grant money to study the ruins and I knew that if I found something," here Julian swept us all with another quick, mortified glance, "something really big, the whole world would know, and then I'd have money pouring in forever. So I... I..." he licked his lips and stuttered to a halt.

"So he forged the calendar at Chichén Itzá," Beau finished for him with spiteful satisfaction. "He made it himself, then he, Billy Joe and I hauled it out there in the middle of the night and buried it near the ruins."

"And later you pretended to find it." Linda carefully avoided looking at Julian. His face was red with shame, and he was studying the toe of his boot intently. I had to look away, unable to bear the moment of his humiliation. Julian finally raised his head to look at us.

"It's all true," he admitted reluctantly. "Beau and Billy Joe helped me with that particular, um, project," he muttered, "and that's why I couldn't say anything when we found the shipwreck They were blackmailing me to keep me quiet."

The plan was to sell the pieces of the wreck," Julian explained slowly. "We found it by accident a couple of months ago when we were trying to salvage a piece of equipment that had fallen off the cliff where we were working."

Two more officers joined us then, carrying radios and maintaining contact with more of their partners above ground. They fell silent after a moment, listening as Julian told us about the cave, and I saw one start taking notes.

"Beau and Billy Joe wanted to sell the contents of the ship ... instead of announcing our ... find," Julian seemed to have difficulty finding the right words. "Beau knew this guy who had money to finance the construction of all of this," Julian waved vaguely at the cave and its trappings, "so we could get the contents of the ship off the floor of the sea without being noticed." He gave me an odd smile, "Probably would have worked too, if it hadn't been for K.C."

"Oh, gosh," I began, on the brink of an apology, but Julian shook his head at me.

"No, don't apologize," he told me gently, "none of this is your fault, K.C. It's been an ugly business all around. I never liked the idea of letting Señor Colón in on the deal but we needed to lease a submersible to reach the ship."

"Wait a minute," Father put in sharply. "Señor Colón? Are we talking about Hernán Colón?" Julian nodded.

"Señor Hernán Colón is involved in this?" one of the policemen asked Julian abruptly. We suddenly had the undivided attention of every single police officer in the cave.

"He's the man."

"But he's in prison," Father said, confused. One of the officers shook his head.

"Not anymore, Señor Flanagan. Señor Colón, how do you say, bust out of jail five days ago with the help of some of his corrupt friends. He is free, but police all over Mexico are looking for him."

"Holy cow!" Father repeated, stunned. He shook his head slowly, looking at me in wonder. "So you really did see him on the yacht that day. It was him all along."

"As I tried to tell you." The thought chilled me to the core. If Colón found out that I'd ruined his operation in Cancún I'd never be safe again. Unless they caught him, that is. "Where is he now?" I asked Julian quickly, "Señor Colón, I mean?"

"He's been moving around a lot, staying aboard his yacht in international waters."

"You will give us a full description of this yacht," Officer Hidalgo suggested firmly to Julian.

"No problem," he said and proceeded to give it, right down to the registration information.

Pretty soon the entire cave was swarming with police. The best part of all was that the whole time Beau had to stand there and watch it happen. I smiled and waved mirthfully at him with a "gotcha" look whenever I caught his eye and eventually he turned his back toward me.

The policemen handcuffed Julian, and motioned him upstairs along with Beau. Father scribbled something on one of his business cards and managed to tuck it into Julian's pocket before the police finally led the three men away.

"If you would be so kind?" One of the other police officers eventually pried Linda away from the crate, telling her that no, she was not allowed to take any pictures of the crime scene and promising her that yes, later she could probably arrange a photo shoot of the Spanish artifacts.

I saw Rudy take one last look out at the sea from the mouth of the cave. Thens we left, and I gratefully accepted his offer to help me up the stairs.

"So they made you jump from there?" he asked me quietly, "and you did it?" I nodded, remembering.

"Kind of like that. There was a crate hanging by a cable, it slammed into the mouth of the cave and began to break. I jumped out, and grabbed onto it —but then it dropped off the bale and we both fell into the water."

"Good thinking, K.C. The crate probably saved your life."

"It probably did," I agreed. We got outside, and saw that the parking lot was occupied by more police. They were taping off the area, so we were asked to leave the premises immediately, and head to the station under official escort. I saw the cute construction worker who had rescued me from the road and gave him a shy smile. He waved and smiled back. Linda hovered at my side as we approached the police car apparently reserved for us.

"K.C., I think we need to get you to a doctor before anyone does any questioning. James?" Father had a brief conversation with Officer Hidalgo who eventually nodded, turning to look at me.

"First you will go to see the doctor, then this afternoon you will come to the police station and make your statement. All right?" I agreed wearily and settled into the back seat of the car. It was crowded but we all managed to squeeze in together. Minutes later I found myself in the emergency room of the local hospital.

I won't bore you with the details, but I got sixteen stitches in my leg and medicated lotion for my abrasions. The doctor sternly advised me to rest and take it easy. I agreed. Father and Linda and Rudy got to their feet as I slowly made my way into the waiting room using the crutches I'd been given. They were tricky but I could manage them if I went very slowly.

We took a taxi back to the hotel where Linda wanted to 'have a look' at my leg. When we got up to our apartment she made me lie down on the bed in my room while she examined me.

"You'll live, K.C.," she told me after making a thorough study of my leg. "Did they give you anything for the pain at the hospital?"

I nodded. "Some tylenol or something."

Linda selected a small tube of salve from the first aid kit, saying, "Let's try some of this." It must have been some kind of topical analgesic, for soon after she had applied it the raw pain in my skin just vanished.

"Thanks," I said, giving the tube of cream a curious glance as I handed it back to her. I couldn't read the label since it was in Chinese.

"Does that feel better?" Linda asked. I nodded, listening to the sounds from the soccer game Father and Rudy were watching in the other room.

"That really helped, the pain is pretty much gone Linda, thanks." It was true my leg didn't bother me very much, but for some reason I felt totally blue. Linda watched me thoughtfully for a moment.

"You seem a little sad, K.C." she remarked quietly. "I bet it was hard finding out that Julian was in on the whole thing." I looked away, unable to meet her eyes for a moment as I nodded. I would never forget my feeling of utter betrayal when he'd turned me over to Beau and Billy Joe.

"Yeah," I muttered, "I really trusted him."

"I know." Linda sounded really disappointed, "me too."

"He saved me, though." I told her, "Beau was about to shoot me and Julian jumped on him." I smiled a little, remembering that part. "It's just so weird, knowing that he can be so cool but so , I don't know, a criminal too. He fooled me, I mean, I really ... I liked him." I colored a little under her gaze at my confession.

Linda tilted her head and raised an eyebrow, telling me, "Well obviously, Julian really likes you too." I looked up at her, startled.

"Really?"

"Well, sure. He must have feelings for you, to have sacrificed himself for your sake, right? I mean, think about it, if he'd just let Beau shoot you, he wouldn't be in jail right now."

"Hmm, that's true," I agreed, feeling a little better. "But I still think the whole thing is weird. I mean, how can you ever really get to know if someone is who they say they are?" Linda gave me a very direct look.

"You're right K.C. It takes a long time to get to know people, and even then they are not always what you might think them to be. It can make life hard on the average person, there's no doubt about that." She finished her sentence quite matter-of-factly.

We sat there in companionable silence for a moment then Linda added, smiling, "Not that your life is what anyone could call average, K.C. I'm beginning to see what James is always talking about."

"What do you mean?"

"You do tend to encounter a lot more, um, weirdness in your life than most people do, haven't you noticed? It's like you have some sort of strange lucky streak. Or else you are just more observant than most people." I smiled a little ruefully.

"Believe me Linda, I do know what you mean."

"And you know, K.C., I want to tell you you were incredibly brave in all of this. Not many kids would have the nerve to jump into the sea like you did. You really are a special young lady."

Father's voice interrupted our tête-à-tête and Linda helped me hobble into the living room. "Are you two talking about what happened? Because if there's an explanation forthcoming I'd really like to hear it."

"K.C. is going to tell us everything," Linda announced, "right from the start." Father and Rudy sank quietly into chairs as I eased my leg before me.

"Topés!" I cried suddenly. "Wait a second, I have to—" I started to climb off the sofa but Rudy held up his hand.

"I'll get her, K.C., Hold on." He was back in a moment with my litle kinkajou. Topés sniffed me curiously then went exploring, prancing along the back of the sofa while I told my family about how I had come to be stuck in a cave with Beau and Billy Joe.

Father scowled disapprovingly a couple of times, especially when he heard about my breaking and entering. I learned that you didn't have to actually *break* anything to be guilty of 'breaking' and entering. I also found out that I could be criminally charged for my trespassing and, believe me, that didn't brighten my day any. Noticing my downcast expression, Rudy spoke up encouragingly.

"Well, look at it this way, who's going to prosecute you?" Rudy asked. "Señor Colón? I think not." The name still made me shiver, and the thought that he was on the run and had me to thank for twice ruining his plans made my hair stand on end.

"Don't worry, K.C., they'll find him," Father assured me confidently. "Julian gave them enough information to nail him for good." He caught our eyes on him and added hastily, "after a fair trial, that is."

"No doubt," Linda nodded, smiling slightly, "and did you hook him up with a good lawyer?"

"A friend of ours from Puerto Vallarta. Julian should be out on bail by tomorrow, latest. Because of his cooperation he'll probably get a lighter sentence and who knows, it might even be reduced to probation with community service," Father finished.

Linda frowned a little and I knew she was thinking that no matter how light his sentence, Julian would lose all the credibility he had in the scientific community. Knowing how important that aspect of his career was to him, its loss was even worse than a jail sentence could ever be.

On the plus side, he had risked his life and sacrificed his career to help me and I blinked tearfully, wondering what would become of him.

"He saved me," I said to Father again. "Beau would have shot me but Julian jumped on him." I felt a sense of remorse that I had inadvertently exposed Julian. I didn't mind bringing Beau and Billy Joe to justice, but Julian was another matter.

"It's not your fault, honey," Linda insisted, sensing my contrition. "You didn't cause any of this mess, you just found out about it."

"As usual." Rudy's remark lacked sting and he cleared his throat awkwardly. "Look, K.C., I'm sorry I was such a jerk about not believing you." I shrugged resignedly.

"It's OK, I understand."

"No, it's not OK," Rudy frowned at me. "If I'd listened to you maybe I could have helped you — instead of your almost getting killed." He shook his head remorsefully, adding, "Anyway, from now on, I promise I'm taking you seriously, OK?"

"OK, Rudy."

"Oh man, what is Pamela going to say?" Rudy ran a hand through his hair, and got to his feet excitedly as though struck by a sudden inspiration. "She'll die when I tell her what happened here." I sighed. The old Rudy was back, or should I say the old *new* Rudy? Anyway, it had been nice while it lasted.

"Say, I think I'll—" he sidled toward the door, reaching for his white panama hat on the hook nearby, "—just go make a quick phone call."

Rudy slapped his hat on his head and bolted out the door. Topés crawled down from my shoulder, curled her tail over her paws, and sat quietly in my lap.

"I think we should go make our statements now, don't you?" Linda suggested, once the dust had cleared from Rudy's departure. Father nodded.

"We'll get this over with as soon as we can, K.C. honey, and then you can come back here and rest."

Giving my statement to the police for the official record wasn't all that bad. It consisted of meeting with

Officer Hidalgo who escorted us all into a large conference room where a young, female typist was waiting to record my words. Officer Hidalgo showed Father, Linda and me to adjoining seats across the table from him and we helped ourselves to ice water from a pitcher on the table.

"Start from the beginning," Officer Hidalgo instructed me just as Linda had earlier. I sighed and began.

It took me a while though, and by the time I reached the end of my tale all the ice in the glass of water on the table before me had melted. Officer Hidalgo fiddled with his notebook, waiting for the typist to record the last part of my statement. His next words took me by surprise. I had expected him to question me further about the discovery of the cave but instead, he brought up the topic of Señor Colón.

"Now think hard, K.C., are you sure Señor Colón did see you?" He asked me this very, very seriously and I nodded my head.

"You know, I really am sure he did, otherwise how can you explain his henchman chasing me through town, and even pursuing me to Chichén Itzá.

"Why do you ask?" I insisted, leaning forward, "do you think he will still come after me, even though the police know about everything now?"

"There is that possibility, *señorita*," Officer Hidalgo replied. "You should be careful, I am sorry to say."

"Have you had any luck in locating Señor Colón's yacht?" Father asked, his tone clipped. Officer Hidalgo glanced swiftly at the motionless policeman guarding the door then nodded slowly.

"*Sí, Señor*, we found the yacht across the bay in Cancún an hour ago and we apprehended several of Señor Colón's crew members, but there was no sign of Señor

Colón himself." His words were followed by utter stillness in the room, then Father exhaled sharply.

"So Colón could be anywhere right now?"

"That is correct, Señor Flanagan." Officer Hidalgo was watching him closely. I saw Father's nostrils flare slightly.

"He could even be right here on this island."

"He could be here, yes."

"We're taking the next flight out of Cancún," Father announced firmly and Linda nodded vigorously.

"That would be best," Officer Hidalgo assured us sincerely. "We will call you as witnesses perhaps later, but for now we can expedite your departure, if you wish."

"Oh yes, we definitely wish." Father replied dryly. I didn't argue. I had no way of knowing whether Señor Colón was around but I sure didn't want to stick around and find out. Leaving Mexico sounded like a good plan to me.

Chapter Seventeen

"It's not that we think anything will actually happen to you, K.C.," Father reassured me as we left the police station. His words might have carried more weight if not for the fact that he was glancing around nervously as he spoke.

"But I'm finished with my research anyway," Linda put in heartily, "and there's no sense staying here any longer if we don't have to. I mean, we don't think that Señor Colón will actually come after you but it's best to be safe, rather than sorry."

Despite their assurances, both Linda and Father were noticeably uneasy about the news we'd received concerning Señor Colón. And so was I. In fact every time I saw a short, heavy-set man on the street, or spotted someone wearing a white suit, I had to fight the urge to scream bloody murder for the police.

"Hey," Rudy glanced up from the book he was reading as we returned. "How did it go?" Father jammed his hands into his pockets and instead of answering, asked a question of his own.

"How would you feel if we left Mexico and returned to Canada early?" he suggested, and Rudy smiled.

"I wouldn't mind, why? How early?"

"Well, tomorrow morning, actually. The police checked with the airlines, the eleven a.m. flight is the only flight to Montreal leaving from Cancún airport tomorrow, and I think we should be on it." Father sounded a little too casual, and Rudy straightened slowly in his chair.

"What happened?" he asked slowly. "What's going on?"

"The police found Señor Colón's yacht and arrested some of his crew members but there was no sign of Colón himself on board," I explained matter-of-factly. "They think he might still be around here, and the police are worried that he'll come looking for me."

"I see," Rudy got to his feet. "Well then, in that case I'll start packing."

"K.C., what are we going to do about Topés?" Linda asked. I shook my head.

"I don't know, I guess I'll have to find someone to take care of her for me." I picked Topés up, cuddling her and stroking her soft orange fur. I really wished I could take her home with me but knew there was no chance I could get away with that. Father would have a fit if I tried to smuggle her through customs back to Canada with me.

I carried Topés with me downstairs, taking the steps slowly with one crutch. When we reached the kitchen Agustín the cook looked up and a big smile lit his face. It faded as soon as he noticed my injuries.

"Señorita, you are OK?"

"Just a little accident," I explained briefly and he waved me into the big kitchen, his eyes twinkling when he saw who I carried with me. "Ah yes, the little kinkajou," he murmured, putting out a finger to stroke Topés' head gently.

As if his words were a cue, two small girls ran out from the pantry and stood there in the middle of the kitchen, looking curiously at me and Topés. One was perhaps eight years old and the other maybe six. Topés sniffed the air delicately in their direction, uncurling her silky tail as she leaned forward. The oldest girl stepped forward a little.

"These are my nieces, Elena and María," the cook introduced us.

"*¡Ay, que bonita!*" Elena reached out a cautious hand to touch Topés. Topés licked her fingers, prompting a quick withdrawal of her hand and a chorus of giggles from both girls.

"Don't worry, she won't bite," I told them. "Would you like to hold her?" Elena nodded vigorously and I handed Topés over. Maria's eyes widened in wonder as she watched her older sister gently pat Topés' small body then she, too wanted a turn to hold the baby kinkajou.

"We're leaving tomorrow," I announced abruptly to Agustín. "I guess I won't be needing any more food for the kinkajou after all."

He frowned. "So soon?"

"There's been a change in plans," I replied. Naturally, I didn't tell him all about Señor Colón, but my vague explanation seemed to satisfy him. We watched as Elena reclaimed Topés, removing her carefully from Maria's chubby grasp.

"What are you going to do with the kinkajou?" she asked shyly, nodding at Topés. I hesitated, then gave her an elaborate shrug, sensing that the solution to my pet problem was about to present itself.

"I'm really not sure, I was going to give her to a friend of mine but he can't take her and now —" I spread my hands sorrowfully and heaved a great sigh, watching Elena from the corner of my eye. "Oh well, I guess I'll think of something." My words seemed to strike a chord with her. Elena shot a pleading look at her uncle and murmured:

"She could stay here, *Tío*. She could live here at the hotel and we will take care of her." María nodded enthusiastically in agreement to this plan and uncle Agustín squinted thoughtfully at the two girls for a moment.

"Why not?" He turned to me with an indulgent smile. "If it pleases you, we will take care of Topés for you. She will be the pet of the Hotel Vista del Mar."

"That's great!" I said with relief. "I was so worried about her, but now I know she'll have a good home." I handed little Topés over to Elena. It was hard to let her go but I knew she'd be happier with them on the island than in any other place I could provide for her.

"Good luck," I whispered to Topés, and I could have sworn she nodded back at me.

"*Gracias, señorita.*" Elena accepted the little animal with gentle awe. "We will take care of her for you. Come back later and see how she grows!"

"Maybe I will, thanks," I smiled. "I have to go pack now. *Adiós.*"

"*Adiós, señorita.*" They waved goodbye to me and after one last lingering look at Topés, I headed upstairs, amazed by my good luck in finding such a nice home for her.

"Where's Topés?" Linda asked when I returned alone.

"The cook's nieces are going to keep her for a pet. She'll live here at the hotel, I guess," I replied.

"That really worked out well, didn't it?" Linda smiled. "I'm sure they'll take excellent care of her and she'll never be hungry again."

We spent the rest of the evening packing and getting ready for our departure the following day. Father and Linda both did everything they could to keep the atmosphere light and tension-free but when Rudy suggested sending out for food instead of leaving the apartment for dinner they both agreed so quickly that I knew they'd been considering it themselves.

I have to admit that I was feeling pretty nervous too. The idea of Señor Colón being somewhere out there and maybe looking for me was far from reassuring. I checked under the bed and locked my windows tight before I went to sleep that night.

The next morning dawned clear and bright, and for once I actually found myself relatively wide awake and ready to go at seven a.m. We checked out of the hotel fifteen minutes later, and headed for the pier where the passenger ferry was due to pick us up at 7:30.

The ferry arrived, and we boarded it carefully, placing our luggage on the long benches beside us. There were only about ten other people with us on the ferry, and they only gave us cursory glances as we settled ourselves comfortably on benches facing the open deck. So far, so good.

"You all right, K.C.?" Father watched as I shifted slightly on the wooden bench, putting my crutches carefully to one side. My leg was still sore, a reminder of my brush with danger, and I glanced warily at all the other passengers on the ferry, studying them all closely to be certain that Señor Colón was not among them.

"I'm fine," I lied, fixing a short skinny man nearby with a piercing stare. Who knew? Colón could have lost a lot of weight since I'd seen him last. Better to be safe than sorry. The man glanced uncomfortably away from my sharp gaze then got up and moved to the opposite side of the ferry.

"Pretty soon we'll be out of here and everything will be all right." Father draped an arm around Linda's shoulder and she smiled up at him. Rudy looked at the two of them together then smiled at his own private daydream.

"Pamela," he murmured langorously. "Just think, in seven hours we'll be together again." I sighed and looked out over the water as the ferry sped us away from Isla Mujeres. The island seemed so small and abstract from this distance that I had trouble believing the events of the last few days had been real.

We took a taxi from the pier to the Cancún airport and from there we went straight through security to the international departures lounge. I didn't feel safe until we were actually seated near the gate, only thirty minutes from takeoff. After checking the surrounding area for suspicious-looking characters and finding none, I sighed with relief and settled into my chair, looking out over the landing strip in anticipation of going home.

That was when I spotted Señor Colón. He was strolling through the terminal in our direction, wearing his trademark spotless white suit and panama hat. He wore dark sunglasses and his face was unshaven but I recognized him from his posture.

Momentarily stunned, I watched as Colón took a seat in a row of chairs near the neighboring departure gate. He tucked a small carry-on bag under the seat next to him. A short fat man in a dusty black suit sitting near him spared him no more than a cursory glance before going back to his newspaper.

"What's wrong?" Rudy asked. Ever since the previous day he had been staying close to my side and keeping an eye on me. He noticed my apprehension right away. Father and Linda were nowhere in sight, they had gone in pursuit of orange juice and were standing in line in front of the bar with their backs to us.

"It's him," I licked my lips and nodded shakily in Señor Colón's direction. "He's sitting right over there." Rudy followed my gaze and his eyes narrowed at the sight of the white-suited man across the waiting area.

"Are you sure it's him?" he asked me a trifle doubtfully and when I shot an indignant glance at him he added, "I'm sorry. Of course it's him. If you say you recognize him that's proof enough for me."

"What should we do? He's obviously planning to leave the country and we have to stop him before he gets away!" I whispered urgently, trying not to stare as the man I'd identified as Señor Colón unfolded a magazine and started flipping idly through the pages.

"Don't worry, K.C.," Rudy said confidently. "I'll take care of this!" Before I could stop him he stood up and strode manfully toward Señor Colón.

"No, Rudy, wait!" I hobbled after him as fast as I could on the crutches.

"Señor Hernán Colón!" Rudy bellowed loudly as he approached the man in white, "you are under arrest for crimes against the Mexican government! Now put that magazine down and get your hands in the air!" Heads turned all over the departure area at his words. The man in white paled a little in the face of Rudy's aggression.

"But —" he began and Rudy repeated:

"I said put the magazine down and get your hands in the air!" A nearby airport security guard looked up at the sound of this commotion then hurried toward us from across the waiting area. The man in the dusty black suit watched his approach nervously through thick-lensed glasses and put his newspaper carefully aside.

"There must be some mistake, Señor." The man in white closed his magazine and carefully placed it on the seat beside him, "I am not —"

"Hands in the air! "Rudy barked again and the man in the white suit, clearly intimidated, did as Rudy had instructed, slowly raising his trembling hands up to the level of his ears.

Black suit looked from Rudy to the approaching security guard then back to Rudy, his eyes glistening behind the thick lenses of his glasses. I saw him glance nervously behind himself towards the boarding gate.

"What seems to be the trouble, Señor?" the airport security guard asked Rudy very politely.

"This man is Señor Hernan Colón, wanted for drug trafficking, money laundering, and other crimes against the Mexican government. Arrest him at once!" Rudy ordered imperiously, pointing at his white-suited prisoner. The airport security guard stared at the man in the white suit in bafflement.

"Arrest him!" Rudy insisted again, glaring impatiently at the security guard.

The man in the black suit got to his feet very casually and raised a handkerchief to his face, apparently blotting the perspiration from his bearded upper lip. I saw a gleam of ruby and gold on the pinky finger of his right hand and gasped in shock, recognizing the ring I'd seen on Señor Colón's hand.

It was then that I realized my error. I'd mistaken the man in white for Señor Colón when the real Señor Colón had been sitting beside him in disguise the whole time. If it hadn't been for the coincidental juxtaposition of the two men I'd never have even recognized the real Señor Colón.

"Omigod, wait, it's *the other one!*" I shouted, pointing with one of my crutches. "That other guy in black, Rudy, *that's* Colón!" At my words, both Rudy and the security guard glanced first at me, then in the direction of my pointing finger.

Under their scrutiny the man in the black suit looked desperately around for an escape route. The only way for him to leave the area was either to climb up and over several rows of benches behind him or to pass right by me.

He chose the latter option, darting forward like the proverbial cornered rat. I swung my left crutch at his foot and tripped him as he tried to scoot past me and into the crowd. He staggered sideways, clutching at one of the security guards to steady himself.

"Stop that man! He's wanted by the Mexican federal police!" I shouted, and the guard's hands instinctively tightened on Señor Colón's shoulders. Just then, Father and Linda returned from their juice-finding mission. Father watched the tableau with considerable astonishment.

"Kids," Father asked, "what's going on?"

Señor Colón straightened up and mustered what he could of his dignity.

"Do not listen to the little girl. She is obviously unbalanced. She attacked me with a stick, did you see her attack me?" He turned indignantly to the security guard holding him, "I demand to be released at once!" Colón's face turned an apoplectic shade of red as the security guard maintained a grip on his arm. "This is an outrage!" he sputtered. "The little girl is obviously insane!"

The other man, the one in the white suit, took advantage of this diversion to grab his carry-on luggage and stroll nonchalantly but rapidly away from this ruckus, unnoticed. Once he was in the clear, he ran for the safety of the crowd and quickly disappeared. No doubt my mistake had left him with an interesting story to tell his family and friends.

"Are you absolutely sure this time that this is Señor Colón?" Father was still eyeing the man in the shabby black suit doubtfully.

"You are making a big mistake," Señor Colón snarled at us, twisting his arm to no avail in the guard's unrelenting grasp. I got a really good close up look at his face for the first time. My arch-enemy was about my height, twice my girth and had a pair of really mean eyes which glared at me from behind thick-lensed glasses. A short, dyed beard concealed his roundish face and from what I could see he didn't have what you could call an attractive smile. Quite the disguise.

"It's him," I told Father with certainty.

"How do you know it's him for sure?" Linda asked. "He doesn't look anything like he did in the newspapers. He's got a beard."

"You thought the other guy was him, too." Rudy reminded me reproachfully and I shrugged apologetically.

"Um, yeah. Sorry about that. But check out the ring on this guy's pinky finger." I pointed to the digit in question, "It's the same one I saw through the binoculars that day. I think I even remember seeing a picture of him wearing it when they arrrested him, I think he always wears it." Señor Colón hastily jammed his ring hand deep into his pocket where we couldn't see it, and his reaction proved my theory.

"See?" I observed, "it's him."

"You have a good eye, K.C." Linda approved. Colón turned a look of utter loathing on me.

"You will regret this, you interfering little bi—."

"Not as much as you will, mister." I replied evenly, cutting off his insult as Father handed one of the airport security guards a business card. "This is the phone number for Officer Hidalgo on Isla Mujeres, he will tell you what has happened and why you should detain this person." The guard squinted thoughtfully from the card to Señor Colón's angry face.

"If you will please wait here quietly, Señor," he said apologetically to Colón, "we will just take a moment to investigate this and then you will be free to go." He pulled out his cell-phone and dialed the number on the business card. *"Sí, Hidalgo, por favor,"* he spoke into the phone quietly.

"Let me go!" Señor Colón began to struggle fiercely with the lone security guard still holding him. The guard hadn't been prepared for a struggle and with the advantage of surprise Colón was able to wrench himself free.

He took off at a heavy run toward the nearest exit. Luckily, two more security guards materialized from nearby and helped the first guard recapture him, pinning him against a soft-drink dispenser while they frisked him from head to foot.

They were too far away for me to hear what anyone was saying at that point but it was just as well since Colón was cursing fluently in gutter Spanish when the two guards brought him back to where we were standing. The security guard who had called Officer Hidalgo for instructions clicked his cell-phone off and turned to Señor Colón with a frown.

"Your identification papers please?" Colón tried to shake off the guards but they held him tightly while searching his jacket pockets. They found the passport in the inside pocket of his vest and brought it out for study under the bright airport lights.

"These are forgeries," one of the guards shook his head soberly. "I am sorry Señor, but we will have to detain you until we can get this situation resolved."

"I want to speak to an attorney at once!" Colón tried bluffing his way out of the situation. "I will not say one word until I have spoken with my lawyer!"

"He's probably waiting for you to show up for your trial, so why don't you go right ahead and give him a call?" I suggested blandly and Colón shot me a malevolent look.

"You are a very nasty little girl!" he told me quite viciously. "You should learn some manners!"

"Oh right, a tip from an expert on courtesy?" I retorted angrily. "A corrupt, drug-smuggling blackmailer?" Colón glared at me speechlessly for a second, groping for words to repay me in kind.

"Someday you will regret what you have done!" he blurted finally. "You will be a very, very sorry little girl! I will see to that!" A fleck of spittle adorned the corner of his mouth and his eyes looked wild.

"The only thing you're going to be seeing is the inside of a jail cell, mister," Rudy remarked with cold certainty.

"Come with us, Señor." All four of the airport security guards seized Colón forcibly, propelling him before them toward their office.

The large crowd of people who had gathered to watch this drama unfold scattered at their approach, and with good reason. As the guards escorted him away, Señor

Colón began to thrash wildly, flinging himself this way and that, kicking and attempting to head-butt anyone who came close to him.

"You cannot do this to me!" he shouted, "I will have your jobs for this! I will file charges, believe me you will never work again!" He looked like an enraged bull and a ripple of involuntary laughter spread through the crowd when he stumbled headlong into a metal ashtray and fell heavily to the ground, still shouting threats at the world and everyone in it.

"Shall we?" Father turned away, glancing at the wall panel announcing our flight. "We'd better start boarding if we don't want to miss our plane."

Epilogue

In the end, the Spanish shipwreck was declared to be a national heritage site and Beau and Billy Joe ended up in a jail near Mexico City, in the same cell block with Señor Colón, the last I heard. Father, Linda, Rudy and I had to fly back down to Mexico to testify at Señor Colón's trial and it was sort of creepy, but worth it, since he won't see daylight again for a long, long time.

I had a lot of time to reflect on what had happened to me. Although the newspapers hailed me as some kind of heroine, I didn't feel much like one, and for some reason my success was not as sweet as it could have been.

I never spoke to Julian again after that last day at the cave, and now and then I wonder how things are going for him. Father helped him get a really good lawyer and Julian got a light sentence which was later reduced to probation. The last I heard he was working for a construction company in Brazil. I like to think that the magic of Ixchel's ruined temple reached Julian in some strange way, breaking him down into pieces, so that he too, just like the temple, could be rebuilt.

Linda wrote her article and sold it to the magazine she works for, *Travel & History*. They liked it so much they immediately assigned her to do a continuation of the story, so in a week she's leaving for Spain to follow up on the story of Francisco Roberto Regalado. I don't think we'll be going with her though. I heard Father speaking to Mother long distance on the phone yesterday, she was in Dallas with her boyfriend Darrell, something about a trip they will be taking to some oil exploration sites he needs to see in Hawaii. Maui, I seem to remember, was the place mentioned. Father hasn't said anything to us yet officially, but he has that strange look he gets when something is going on. I guess I'll know soon enough.

The weirdest thing happened when we got back to Montreal. Rudy went out with Pamela only three more times, and then he broke up with her. I wonder if it was the opera that did it after all? Anyway, Pamela is dating a football player now and seems to have fully recovered from her heartbreak. Rudy has dated around some since then but is still mostly single. It's a nice change.

I have a cool scar on my right leg to remind me of Isla Mujeres and some pretty interesting memories of the Yucatán. I think I'll go back when I'm studying for my archeology degree. After all, Julian said there were dozens of Mayan sites left to be rediscovered. Maybe I'll be the one who finds them. And who knows, maybe I'll see my little Topés again!

Anyway, despite all the excitement I remembered to keep this travel diary and I hope you enjoyed hearing all about my adventures. Thanks for tuning in! If you ever want to see my pictures of Cancún, Isla Mujeres and Chichén Itzá, I posted them up on the web, and of course I have e-mail.

Just connect to http://www.rdppub.com/KookCase.

¡See ya!
K.C.

Here is an excerpt from the first novel in the

K.C. Flanagan, girl detective™ series,

PANIC IN PUERTO VALLARTA.

Suddenly, a door slammed across the street and I looked own to see a man dressed in khaki pants and a white shirt emerge from the lobby of the hotel across the street. I watched him curiously because he glanced furtively this way then that before heading out on foot past the musicians.

I studied him closely, intrigued by his sneaky demeanor and was surprised to see him suddenly turn around and dart back towards the hotel from which he had just emerged. The reason for his abrupt change of direction became apparent as a sedan pulled up to the curb behind him and a wiry man in a dark suit emerged from the car, shouting what must have been his name.

The first man didn't respond to this hail, but instead quickened his pace. Not fast enough though, for the guy in the suit caught up to him as he was nearing the door of the hotel and roughly put a hand on his arm to detain him. They scowled at each other and I saw the man in the khakis try to pull free. The wiry man in the dark suit leaned in closer, saying something which made the first man glance around himself in panic.

The encounter between the two men was undoubtedly not one of old friends, for although they obviously knew each other there was something quite sinister about the way the guy in the suit was leaning over the first man. In fact there was something downright threatening about the way he was detaining the man in the khaki pants. My hotel travel magazine lay forgotten in my lap as I watched the scene below me unfold.

I glanced across the balcony toward Father and Rudy's room, hoping to see one or the other of them there only to find that I was alone. The musicians on the street below played on, oblivious to the drama behind them. I watched with concern as the door to the sedan opened and yet another man stepped out to join the scenario.

The second man from the car wore dark blue dress slacks with casual shoes and a polo-necked white cotton shirt with the sleeves rolled up to his elbows. I couldn't see his face at all but his build was muscular and his body seemed perfectly proportioned. When he moved he kept his head down. Together the two men escorted the man in the khakis roughly back toward the inside of the hotel.

I kept watching the entrance to the hotel across the street for several minutes, hoping to see them all emerge safely, having resolved their differences when instead, to my alarm, I heard a shout and the sound of breaking glass quite clearly even above the serenade below.

I looked up and directly across the narrow street to the balcony of the hotel opposite me. A sliding door opened and the man in khakis stumbled out, clutching at the narrow iron railing as if for support. His nose, which had been fine when I'd seen him last, was flattened and smeared with red. Blood had run down from his face onto his white shirt and he was sporting a wicked-looking bruise over his left eye.

He looked as though he had been on the receiving end of a not-so-welcoming committee. I stood up, leaning forward as though there were something I could do to help him. He glanced across at me and for a brief moment his eyes met mine. I was appalled by the look of desperation I saw there.

Then the guy in the dark suit joined him on the balcony and punched him again, this time right in the mouth. The man in khakis toppled over sideways onto a potted palm then slid to the tiled floor of the balcony in a heap of bloodstained clothing.

Now, I guess this is where the story really begins because I found myself shouting, "Hey! Stop it!" at them, trying hard to make myself heard over the performance below. Dark Suit looked up at the sound of my voice and for a long moment we studied each other. I was particularly chilled by the flat expression on his face.

I mean, there was no anger or rage in him, none of the usual passion which accompanies an act of violence, yet I had just seen him beat someone to a pulp. He seemed oddly detached for his circumstances and I felt a flash of fear as he scowled at me then turned back to the man in khakis.

In one smooth move the man in the dark suit leaned down and hoisted his victim more or less to his feet then dragged him inside the hotel room where the other man waited, back behind the curtains. I watched, white knuckled, as Dark Suit pulled the filmy blue and white striped curtain completely closed across the balcony windows as if to block my view of what occurred next.

What he didn't take into account was the fact that the sun had set over the ocean, a glorious display of rich reds and oranges (had I been in a mood to appreciate it) and dusk was falling. Despite the drawn curtains I could see the three of them plainly silhouetted against the material and I could perfectly observe what happened.

The man in the khakis pulled drunkenly away and stood there, his shadow swaying across the light from the room and then Polo Shirt brought something heavy down on his head in a blow which was meant to crush. The man in the khakis went down and never got up again. I stood there stunned for a split second then someone turned out the lights and the room across the street was plunged into darkness.

"Buenas noches, K.C.," Rudy greeted me cheerfully as he joined me on the balcony. "Man, those guys really get into their work, don't they?" I stared at him, horrified, wondering how he could be so callous, until I realized that he was referring to the musicians below us. I licked my lips. "What's the matter?" Rudy asked solicitously. "You look like you've seen a ghost." His words were lighthearted yet uncannily accurate and I nodded.

"I just saw a man killed," I told him, trying not to let my voice quaver. "I think I'd better call the police." Rudy gazed at me in astonishment.

"Killed? Where?"

"Over there." I pointed across to the balcony which was now dark and quiet. To my surprise my hand was trembling and I withdrew my pointing finger as soon as I noticed this, hoping that Rudy hadn't. "They were there, I swear it!" I insisted. Rudy stared across at the quiet balcony then back at me as he sighed.

"Now K.C. If you'll forgive my mentioning it, you do have a tendency to over-exaggerate things," he told me condescendingly. I scowled at him in protest, my alarm turning to annoyance at his refusal to believe me.

"I do not," I objected.

"You do so," he insisted mildly. I shook my head, about to explain how wrong he was but he held up a hand, assuming the Stance of The Older Brother. "What about that time in the Grand Canyon? You went and got yourself lost in the canyon all because you thought you were following an escaped prisoner. Remember?"

"But I was following an escaped prisoner! And because of me we caught him!" I retorted, affronted that he would dismiss my accomplishment so easily. "But that's not important right now." I turned on my heel, away from Rudy's disbelief and headed for the phone in the room. "I just saw them kill a man! I can't just sit here and do nothing." I studied the list of important numbers by the phone. Good, there it was, the number for the state police, 3 25 00.

"What's up?" Father came into my room, glancing from Rudy to where I stood clutching the phone with a frown. "Are you all right?" I shook my head.

"I just saw a man killed," I told him without preamble and Father's eyebrows shot up in surprise.

"You did? Where?" I pointed to the darkened hotel room across the street. Father quickly crossed the room to peer at it from my balcony, as I had done just minutes before.

"There's nothing there," he informed me and I shrugged impatiently.

"Well, not now there isn't, but there was. They turned out the lights right after they whacked him over the head," I said tersely, starting to dial.

"Are you absolutely sure?" Father's expression was serious, his normally good-natured smile replaced by a look of true concern. "Are you sure you didn't make a mistake? K.C., stop a minute and think." I hesitated and turned toward him, my glance falling on the street below where the musicians were packing it in for the evening.

If I hadn't been looking out at that moment I would have missed it. The man in the dark suit emerged from the hotel lobby, staggering toward the car he had left parked so haphazardly by the curb. I say 'staggered' because he and the man in dress slacks supported the limp body of the man in khakis, and it looked to me like the khaki guy was a dead weight. Literally.

Although it might have seemed to the casual observer that the man in khakis was walking I could see that his feet simply trailed behind him on the ground. I dropped the phone and leaped across the room to the window, shouting,

"There they are!" All three men were wearing hats but I recognized their clothing. "That's them!" I shouted, leaning over the edge of the balcony.

The man in the dark suit, the one I had locked gazes with earlier, looked up and saw me staring and pointing at him. His face flushed with anger then he leaned across to speak to the man in slacks who didn't look up and they both quickened their pace, heading for the sedan.

"Someone stop them!" I shouted again, more loudly. Heads turned all up and down the street to stare at me, and the musicians all turned to look in the direction of my pointing finger. For a moment they regarded the three men passing them in utter silence then they burst into laughter. I saw one of them make a tilting motion with his hand to his mouth, as though he held a mug of beer and they all laughed again.

"K.C., calm down," Father told me gently. "It looks as though he might have had too much to drink and passed out. See? They're probably just helping him get home safely." I scowled at him and he sighed. "You must try to stop letting your imagination get the better of you." Draping a firm arm across my shoulder, Father steered me inside the room and away from the balcony. "Now let's all calm down, shall we?" I peered over my shoulder at the sedan in time to see it pull away from the curb and head down the street. It was too dark for me to make out the license plate number.

"Kook Case," Rudy muttered under his breath as he dropped into a chair by the desk in my room.

"I heard that!" I scowled blackly at him, showing my disapproval of this perversion of my nickname. "I didn't make it up. I know what I saw and I'll find a way to prove it, Rudolph," I insisted, deliberately using his full name. Rudy frowned and opened his mouth, no doubt to retaliate in kind.

"All right, all right." Father held up a placating hand to prevent any further exchange of pleasantries between his beloved children. "Let's all just sit down and take it easy. I'll call down to the front desk and ask them to check on it." After he made the call, I allowed him to provide me with a can of chilled cola from the small refrigerator in my room and sat down on the bed to sip it, studiously ignoring Rudy.

Rudy and Father are both great, I mean I wouldn't trade them for any other family in the world but sometimes they have an appalling lack of faith in me. Just because I happen to be more observant than them, and just because I like to follow up on the things I see and find out what's actually going on in the world around me they lecture me about being nosy or interfering. I've learned that at times like this it does me no good to argue and so I subsided into dignified silence, pondering what I had seen.

"K.C.'s sulking," Rudy remarked eventually.

"I am not," I retorted, "I'm thinking." Father sighed and stood up as the phone rang. He picked up the receiver, and said, "Yes? Yes, no, no. Yes, I see." Then he said to me, "K.C., they sent a man to ask outside. What you saw was just a couple of drunks on the street. Really, sweetheart, that's all it was."

"I'm thinking I'm going to turn in, kids. Tomorrow is going to be a busy day. You two behave yourselves, all right?" with which words of adult advice he left us.

Rudy parked himself in the chair across the room, playing fast and loose with the remote control, rapidly switching channels back and forth on the television set the way he does when he's trying to annoy me, one instant on basketball, the next, on some sitcom, then back to sports. Finally I told him that I, too, was planning to get some sleep and he left.

But it wasn't until two or three in the morning that I actually did get to sleep. Every time I closed my eyes I saw the bright splash of blood on the face of the man in khakis and remembered the look on his face as he'd searched for an escape route. When I eventually dreamed, it was about being chased by sinister strangers carrying guitars which they fired at me like guns as I fled through unending darkness, unable to get away.

If you don't live near a bookstore, you can order K.C. Flanagan books from the publisher by mail or fax, (using the following order form, and paying by check or Visa/Mastercard), or from the K.C. Flanagan Internet site on the World-Wide Web at http://www.rdppub.com/KookCase, (credit cards only).

Please mail to
Robert Davies Multimedia Publishing Inc.,
330-4999 St. Catherine St.,
Westmount, Quebec, Canada H3Z 1T3
or Fax to 514-481-9973

PLEASE SEND ME:

QTY	TITLE	PRICE	POSTAGE	TOTAL
	PANIC IN PUERTO VALLARTA	$8.99 CAN $5.99 US	$2	
	CHAOS IN CANCÚN	$8.99 CAN $5.99 US	$2	
			GRAND TOTAL	

NAME	
ADDRESS	
CITY–PROV./STATE	
POSTAL CODE/COUNTRY	
CHECK INCLUDED FOR $_____ OR	
VISA/MASTERCARD #	EXP.